5.1-06

A True and Faithful Narrative

By Katherine Sturtevant

At the Sign of the Star
A True and Faithful Narrative

KATHERINE STURTEVANT

A True and Faithful Narrative

FARRAR STRAUS GIROUX
NEW YORK

www.fsgkidsbooks.com

Library of Congress Cataloging-in-Publication Data
Sturtevant, Katherine.
    A true and faithful narrative / Katherine Sturtevant.— 1st ed.
        p.   cm.
    Summary: In London in the 1680s, Meg—now sixteen years
old—tries to decide whether to marry either of the two men who
court her, taking into account both love and her writing ambitions.
    ISBN-13: 978-0-374-37809-7
    ISBN-10: 0-374-37809-6
        1. London (England)—History—17th century—Juvenile fiction.
[1. London (England)—History—17th century—Fiction.   2. Great
Britain—History—Charles II, 1660–1685—Fiction.   3. Authorship—
Fiction.   4. Courtship—Fiction.   5. Sex role—Fiction.]   I. Title.

PZ7.S94127Tru 2006
[Fic]—dc22

                                                            2005046922

For Peter Szego,
with love and thanks

1681

One

He came to see me before he sailed for Italy.

It was toward the end of Lent, not many weeks past my sixteenth birthday. I was not expecting to see him, and did not understand, at first, why he had come. I thought he meant to buy a book, and then, when I saw him draw a folded note from the pocket of his bright green waistcoat, I supposed he was there to deliver a message from his sister, Anne, who was my dear friend. But he had come for another reason.

Later, when we heard what befell him, I remembered certain things: the colors of his clothes, the way the spring air had chilled his nose to brightness, how the sea-coal glowed in the grate, and the scents of turpentine and lavender wafting up from my apron. I remembered, too, the softness of his fingers as he put his shillings upon my palm, and the way he let his hand linger on mine.

There I stood, mouth agape, and knew not what to say.

But before that came the argument with my father. We were only four at breakfast, and that counted Deb, the chambermaid, who always sat with us at table. My father's apprentice had already opened the bookshop, and the little ones ate with Bridget, the nurse. I was reading a story which Mademoiselle de Scudéry had written, and had brought it with me to the dining room. There I sneaked glances at it lying open in my lap while I drank my chocolate and ate a bit of cold sparrow pie. It was a thrilling tale, filled with all manner of perils: storms, shipwrecks, pirates, and many abductions of the heroine, Mandane, by her daring suitors. I had quickly seen that she would always remain true to Cyrus, her beloved, but in spite of that I picked up the book every chance that came, and could hardly wait to learn what I already knew.

At first I paid little heed to what was said as I ate. I seldom did, for our talk at table was often dull. Susannah, who had been my father's wife nearly four years, was kind in her way, but she was greatly more interested than I in how to relieve the pain of a baby who cuts his first milk tooth, and what will best protect a tapestry from moths. Useful knowledge, I allow, but lean subjects for conversation. That day Susannah and Deb rattled on about how greatly new hangings were needed in the parlor. In a little while, Betty, the cook-maid, brought in some bread and butter, and then left again. At last Susannah asked my father how his business did, and that was when I looked up from my story.

"Well enough," he answered her. "But I have resolved that I will not publish Mr. Phillips's account of Lord Stafford's execution, after all."

"I'm glad to hear it," Susannah said. "The tide is turning in this business of the Catholics, and I know not whom 'tis more dangerous to offend. Silence is surely the wisest course."

My father's jaw tightened with displeasure. "That is not my reason," he said. "There is more to be considered when publishing a book than who will be offended. Mr. Phillips made a fine story of the affair while we were at cards one night; I felt sure that what he wrote would be worth reading. But the thing is all a muddle, and peppered with lies throughout."

I saw that this was the chance I had been dreaming after day and night. "Can it not be written over, by someone with greater art?" I asked. "I know that sometimes you have put the stories of others into your own words."

"I have not the time," he said, but he began to chew more slowly, as though he was thinking it over.

I judged the moment ripe. "Then let me do it, Father! You know I'm forever busy with my quill. I will fix the muddle."

I saw from his glance that he was both surprised and troubled, but all he said was, "Nay, Meg. This is not women's work."

"*Please*, Father. I am well practiced."

"It is serious business, Daughter. The censor will go over every word."

"If you would but look at some of the things I have written—"

"I don't need to look at them. Give me their titles; that will be enough."

I sat still for a moment, thinking of titles that might surprise and impress him: *Discourse on the Duties of Children Toward Their Parents*, perhaps, or *Reflections on the Sermons of Reverend Little.*

"A title, Meg. The things you write have titles, I presume? What is your latest?"

"*A Maid's Secret: Relating . . .*" Then I faltered.

"Relating?" my father prompted.

I took a breath and spoke quickly and loudly. "*Relating the Strange and Wonderful Events That Befell a Virgin in Faraway Lands, and How She Escaped Her Evil Captors.* And 'tis very good! Much better than some of the stories we sell here in the shop!"

"Margaret! You are immodest," Susannah said.

"However good or bad it may be, it does not fit you for the sort of writing that must be done to publish Mr. Phillips's account," said my father. "Mr. Barlow, however, might try his hand at it." Will Barlow was my father's apprentice.

"Will! You think that Will is more fit for this task than I am? You think that *Will* is more serious than I am?"

"Hold your tongue, Meg," Susannah said sharply.

"Will stays up until one in the morning playing cards at the tavern night after night!"

My father slammed his spoon against the table. "Stop this racket at once!" he said. "Quarrels are not salutary for a woman in Susannah's condition."

Silence fell upon us all. I looked at Susannah, but she did not look at me. Instead she lifted a corner of her apron and examined it, as though she saw a stain. She was with child, then. Again.

I mumbled my congratulations, and Susannah nodded her thanks. After that I said nothing more, and as soon as I dared, I rose to leave the table. Just then, however, little Toby came running into the dining room.

"Meg!" he called out as he ran to me, and I took him into my arms without thinking. Mine was the warm body he knew the best, for we had shared a bed since his baby sister, Eleanor, was born.

"He is always running from his nurse," my father said with a frown.

Toby clung to me and whispered into my neck, "You must take me to the house of office, Meg. Bridget makes me go alone!"

"The woman is too harsh with him," Susannah said, not for the first time.

"We must not indulge him this way, or he will never learn to obey her," my father replied.

"Bridget hits me, always!" Toby cried out as I set him down. "I hate her! I wish that she may grow a long beard!"

"Be silent, Child!" my father shouted. "Mind your tongue and mend your ways, or I will be the one who does the hitting!" Then he spoke more quietly. "Listen to me, Tobias. You must never, never wish ill upon another, for you know not what harm may come of it."

"Surely it was only a childish fancy," I said.

"You, Margaret, of all people, ought to know what power lies in words. Why are we forbidden to curse, if curses are feeble and impotent? Speech is a weighty business."

"Yes, sir," I said obediently, for I had angered my father enough that morning. But I thought to myself that it would be difficult indeed to know if a hard fate had come through ill wishing or through some other cause.

When my father had gone to the bookshop, I took Toby by the hand and led him to the house of office, which was in the basement. Of course he did not like to go alone, for it was dark and the smell from the vault was foul. I well remembered the first time my own nurse had made me go there by myself, but I could not recall how old I had been. It was true that Toby was somewhat overtimid, and we were all a little anxious about it. But he would not grow more brave from Bridget's cuffs.

I waited while he sat on the close-stool, and when he was done I emptied the pan into the vault, where the night-soil waited to be taken away by the cart. Then I sent Toby back to Bridget, hoping she would think he had gone by himself, after all.

2

That morning it was my task to oil the furniture in the parlor, which Deb had dusted before breakfast. Susannah made the oil from candle ends and turpentine, and added a bit of lavender to sweeten the air. I began with the hinged table that my father sat at when he studied manuscripts. My mind was free to wander as I worked, and at such times I often thought about the stories I was writing, and how I might better what I had done. But this morning I was still stinging from my father's scorn, and all I could think of as I slid my oily rag across the table was that it was Will Barlow's fault. When Robert Barnes had been chief apprentice my father was glad to have a daughter with a sharp mind and a ready tongue, but when my father signed Will Barlow in Robert's place, things changed. Will was quick and clever, and my father valued him above any apprentice that had ever been bound to him. But being clever in business did not mean that he was skilled with words, and I felt certain that I could do more justice than Will to the account of Lord Stafford's execution.

I finished the table and knelt beside the walnut armchair so that I would not have to stoop to reach the carving on its back. As I followed the scrollwork with my rag, I thought again of what my father had said, that Mr. Phillips told a fine story, but that the manuscript was riddled with lies. What was the difference, finally, between a story and a lie? It was something I had pondered before. Reverend Little preached that we lie from greed and from fear, but he said naught of stories. Madame Clarke, who had been my teacher, told me that stories carry truth in their message, though their particulars may be invented.

"Like the story of Dick Whittington, who came to London with nothing but his cat and became Lord Mayor?" I asked her.

"Nay, Meg, that is no moral tale but a sop to hungry apprentices."

"Like the story of the apprentice who fought ten Turks single-handed, and vanquished them all?"

"Like the stories in the Bible," Madame Clarke said, opening that book.

"We are not going to study the Bible yet again?" I asked in dismay.

I was two years in Herefordshire, studying with Madame Clarke. Besides my catechism, she taught me how best to carve a hen and to make a mulberry jelly, though I cannot say I learned her lessons well. I was not an earnest pupil. How could it have been otherwise, with me so many miles from London, from family and friends, from news and gossip and all that made life dear to me? In Herefordshire there was naught to do but study, and take long walks among the fruit trees, and listen to Madame Clarke's brother preach at the village church. When the boredom of it all overcame me it was not unnatural that I should torment my teacher a little, and I know not who was the gladder when I finished my studies at last, and was returned to my father's bookshop, at the sign of the Star in Little Britain Street.

And yet I knew that Madame Clarke had done me no small service, for besides the stories from the Bible she taught me the ones told by the Greeks and the Romans, and sometimes, after my French lesson, we studied Latin, though my father had said it was not good for girls. He did not think the classics a proper subject for those of the female sex, lest it make them unfit for marriage.

The very word *marriage* made my jaw grow tight. I gave the chair leg one last rub and yanked my rag back. Then I went to the oaken settle that stood against the wall and attacked it as though it were a traitor to the realm. I hated to think of marriage, and for long months I did not let the idea of it enter my brain, but now Susannah's unwelcome news had brought it to mind once more.

I could not help wishing she had not conceived again so soon. With each new baby came more changes. Already we had one apprentice instead of three, for we had not the space to house three, nor the wherewithal to feed them. Now children slept where once servants had, and servants where apprentices had lain, and I did not know where we would put another body, however little it might be.

But all that was nothing compared to the real matter, which was my father's property, and the way my share of it grew smaller with each birth. Before my father remarried I had not worried about my future, for I was his heir then, and likely to have my pick of many eager suitors. But now little Toby would inherit the business, and if I did not marry soon, my father's fortune would be so many times divided that nothing would remain for my dowry.

"You are needed in the shop, madame," Deb said from the doorway. "I'm to finish in here."

I straightened to look at her, much surprised. It was rare that I was asked to help with the business before dinner. Generally my father kept the shop in the morning, and sent Will to do his errands. But I learned nothing from staring at Deb's round face except that she was resentful, for which I did not blame her, for now she must do my work and her own as well.

"Do you know why my father has summoned me?" I asked.

"Mr. Moore has gone out. 'Tis Mr. Barlow who begs your assistance."

Now *that* was surely a lie. Will Barlow never begged for anything.

3

The shop was my favorite place in all the world. From a child I had loved everything within: the oaken counter, the gleaming wooden floors, the wainscoted walls. I loved the fireplace surrounded by Delft tiles the color of cream, and the four cane chairs grouped before it, where poets and playwrights, physicians and philosophers sometimes sat and argued. Most of all, of course, I loved the books, from the unbound pages that lay upon the table to the volumes with gilded leather covers that were hid on shelves behind curtains to keep them from the black soot that sifted through the air.

There were no customers in the shop when I entered, which surprised me. "Why, nothing is stirring," I said, looking around. "What help can you need from me?"

"Your father asked me to look over a manuscript this morning," Will answered. "You will mind the counter while I read."

I felt my anger rising, and wrestled with it as I might with a dog that snatched a joint of beef from the table. Will didn't need my help; he might as easily have read between customers, as I often did. He sought only to give me orders that I must follow whether I would or no. I saw that he was watching me, the way he always did, to see if he had struck a spark with the flint of his command. There was something in him that seemed to take satisfaction in seeing me lose my temper, which was why I fought to keep it. So I did not answer him, but only took my place behind the counter, while he went to a chair by the fire, stuck out his long legs, and began to study Mr. Phillips's story. He was the sort of youth who is careless with his posture and careful of his clothes. The curls of his wig were inky black, and his moustache was brown with a hint of red. But it was his little mouth I most disliked, for it often bore a mocking smile, and I sometimes feared I was the one it mocked.

I had Mademoiselle de Scudéry's romance with me, and at once I settled into reading it, but after a very few minutes he began to pester me.

"This is a sorry piece of work," he said.

I made no answer.

"Strange that he does not write better; over a pint of sack he is a great wit."

"Perhaps he did not drink enough sack while he was writing."

"Too much drink is more likely to harm prose than to help it," he said.

"You know more of drink than I."

After that he didn't speak for a few minutes. I took great satisfaction in having silenced him, and at the same time wished he would speak again, and say more of what he read.

By and by my wish came true. "This is dull as river rock," he said. "No wonder your father wishes me to try my hand at it. I wager I can liven it a little."

I almost told him I would take that wager, but managed to keep a latch upon my tongue.

Then he said, "What book is that?" And without waiting for my reply he continued, "You read more than anyone I ever saw."

"Not more than my father."

"He is a man—and a bookseller."

"I am a bookseller as well."

He did not contradict me, but smiled in a pitying way that made me want to pull the hairs from his moustache. "When I have my own shop I will not sell such things as this," he said. "There is too much risk of offense."

"Not every bookseller has courage enough to speak the truth," I allowed.

But he did not rise to my bait. "A merchant must always be prudent if he expects to stay in business." I made no reply, and he continued, "When I have my own shop I will not sell so many plays and verses."

"Because few buy them, I suppose?"

"To be sure."

"Yet someone must publish them."

"Someone always will. And you, if you had the running of a bookshop, what would you sell there?"

I was so surprised that I stared, and then set my volume upon the counter that I might think. "I would certainly sell plays, and poetry, and heroic romances set in foreign lands. And I would publish essays, and works on scientific subjects, and arguments about whether women should be taught Latin. And many, many sermons and books of devotion, far more than we offer here, for nothing sells as well."

"In other words, you wish to sell everything! You are like your father."

"If my father knew your views I'm sure he would mend his ways."

I did not suppose that I could make him blush, but I thought he would close the conversation, and then I would be free to return to Mandane's adventures. He only laughed, however. "Every apprentice ponders what he would do differently."

"I don't think my father has done so badly. He has published John Dryden, who is the most famous playwright living. Only last year he published a learned treatise by Mr. Boyle on chemical principles. And of course he reprints many classical works. People will always buy Latin books."

"Yes, Latin works are of great use to learned men."

"Perhaps they will someday be of use to learned women."

"I suppose *you* believe that women should be taught Latin?"

"I do not think it should be forbidden."

"I do. A woman who has the learning of a man can never be happy submitting to her husband's authority."

"That is what Anne's father said on St. Valentine's Day when I dined with the family, which made me laugh, for Mr. Gosse asks his wife's approval in every small thing! There have been fishwives with not one word of Latin who ruled their husbands, and ladies who could translate Ovid who did their wifely duties humbly. The man who will not admit the truth of that is either a dunce or a hypocrite."

I meant the remark for Will, but he turned it neatly. "And did you call Mr. Gosse a dunce at his own table?"

I paused a moment, to choose my words. "I did not say that, exactly. But he understood my views well enough."

"And did you persuade him to your cause?"

"Of course not. If men were as easy to persuade as that, women would be masters of all ancient tongues by now! But Anne's brother Edward took my part."

Just then a customer entered, or so I thought. I felt a presence at the door—I cannot say I saw him, for I was not looking that way, but some small sound or moving shadow caught my notice. We turned, both of us, and Edward Gosse, whose name had been that moment on my lips, came into the shop.

For an instant I did not know him. When I had dined at Anne's on the day that was both my sixteenth birthday and St. Valentine's Day, he had worn his own fair hair about his shoulders. After dinner Mr. Gosse played the fiddle and we danced, and I watched his curled locks bounce around his laughing face. But since then he had bought himself a wig, one of the very large ones crowded with false curls that near doubled the size of his head, and he was dressed like a gentleman in a bright green waistcoat and a suit of figured silk. He wore a sword with a silver hilt at his side, and on his head a beaver hat adorned with feathers. He looked almost elegant, and I saw that a girl who did not know him so well as I might even think him handsome.

"Why, Edward, have you dressed up in your father's things?" I asked. "Or was he made a knight, that you are clothed so fine?" Edward colored, and Will threw his gaze upward, and I wished my words unspoken.

"I hope your family are well?" Will asked with great civility.

"Very well, thank you," Edward replied. He began to look around the shop, while one hand played awkwardly with the strings of his neckband.

"Do you look for something particular?" Will inquired.

Edward picked up a pamphlet and read off the title. " '*Reasons of the Increase of the Dutch Trade.*' This is Roger

Coke's work against the Navigation Acts, is it not?" he asked Will.

"Yes, and powerfully written."

"And do you hold his view? Because you must allow that the Navigation Acts have been very good for the Atlantic trade."

I took up my book again and started to read. If either of them had asked my opinion I would have said that there could be no duller subject for a book than the laws governing commerce, but I knew my views were not wanted in a conversation between two someday-merchants. I paid no more heed to them as they spoke, for Cyrus was fighting a duel that required my whole attention. I was so enthralled by my history that Will had to call my name twice before I lifted my head.

"I must get on with my work," he said. "If you will mind the shop, madame, I will do my reading within." And he left me alone with Edward.

I pulled the ledger from beneath the counter so that I could record his purchase, then saw that he had nothing in his hand. Before I could ask him what he had come for, and why he had not left, a man entered the shop looking very hurried. "Is this where William Okeley's narrative is sold?" he asked without a greeting. "The man that was captured by Barbary pirates and enslaved in Algiers?"

"Nay, you will find that book at the sign of the Peacock, in Chancery Lane, near to Fleet Street," I told him with regret, and he turned on his heel and went out again.

"These narratives of captivity are always popular," I

said to Edward, but he paid no heed, for he was ready at last to tell me why he had come.

"I have brought you a message from Anne," he said, and reached inside his waistcoat to take out a folded paper.

I read it as he watched me. She had written only two lines: *Edward has news for you. Be kind to him.*

I put the note upon the counter and turned to him, bewildered. I imagined that he had brought evil tidings that oppressed his spirits and would now oppress mine, but I could not fathom what they might be. "Edward, what is it?" I asked.

"I'm sailing for Livorno, in Tuscany," he said. "The city we in England call Leghorn. Mr. Nicholson sends me to be his factor there. I will represent him in all his business dealings."

"Why, that is very pleasing news! What luck for you! I have always longed to travel to the Mediterranean."

"It is a rare opportunity. Livorno is like the center of the world; there are merchants there from all lands."

"And you are so young—you have hardly begun the third year of your apprenticeship. Now I understand your finery: you must reflect well upon your master. How did he come to choose you for such important duties?"

" 'Tis my gift with foreign tongues. I can converse in Italian, French, and Spanish."

"Well, that is nothing wonderful. They are all made from Latin, after all."

· He paused for only a moment, then spoke in a voice that mocked, though gently. "You are right, of course. It is almost a cheat to call them three languages instead of one. Still, Mr. Nicholson could find no one abler to send in my stead. I hope to study Arabic while I'm there; it is very useful in that region, but learning it will be a greater trick. *You are fluent in all, I suppose?*"

Now it was I who blushed. I had meant to display my own learning, not to belittle his. "I have only enough French to entertain myself," I said, gesturing at my book. "I didn't mean—Mr. Nicholson is fortunate to have an apprentice skilled in foreign tongues. I'm very pleased for you, Edward."

"There is—there is a reason I would rather not leave just now."

"Of course: you will miss Anne's wedding!"

He smiled as though I had said something very funny. "Yes, 'tis a great pity."

"And when do you sail?"

"Tomorrow morning. I have already taken leave of my family."

"So soon! How can you be ready?"

"Can you offer me something that will make me more ready?"

I heard his voice alter, but I paid no heed; instead I pondered his words. Books were indeed very necessary on a voyage at sea. "We have an account of travels in the Mediterranean you may like to read on the journey," I said. "Or there is a heroic romance set in Granada during the time of the Moors; it has not been Englished, but we have the French. I believe you would enjoy it, and 'tis long enough to keep you occupied for many hours."

"I will buy the book about Granada," he said.

I saw that he was smiling again. When he smiled he looked more like Anne's brother, the boy I had known since I was twelve. "You are lucky; it comes already bound," I said, and went to fetch the volumes—there were six of them.

"And perhaps some verse," Edward said. "The Latin writers, as I'm going to Italy. I have lately been wanting to enjoy the love poems of Catullus again—have you read them?"

I turned to look at him, surprised and confused. Why did he imagine it possible that I had read works written in a classical tongue? I wondered if Anne had revealed to him that I had learned Latin without the knowledge or consent of my father. As it happened, I had not read the poems of Catullus, for Madame Clarke kept to Cicero's speeches, and other things of that sort. But this was not something I could say to Edward.

He did not turn his gaze from mine as he took the books I held and placed them on the counter.

"My father does not print Catullus," I said at last.

"Ah. A pity," he replied.

"You must bring Anne a splendid wedding present when you return," I said as I opened the ledger. "Only think of the treasures you can buy for her in the Mediterranean!"

He pulled off his lace-trimmed gloves and laid them on the counter. "It will likely be a year, perhaps two, before I come again to England," he said as he brought out his purse.

"To be sure. I had not thought. Well, you must send her something, then. Venetian lace, perhaps. Anne would love that."

He fished out his shillings, and put them into my open palm. His fingers were warm and soft. Before I could curl my hand around the coins he laid his own palm over mine, trapping the money between our two hands. "And what shall I bring you, Meg?"

It was then that I remembered Anne's words, *Be kind to him*, and understood them for the first time. My mouth fell open and I was flooded with horror, for it was clear that he offered me a courtship gift. I knew not what to say, and it is a fault of mine that I cannot be still at such moments. Instead, the wrong words fly from my tongue.

"Why, nothing, unless—yes, I so wish we had a narrative to rival Okeley's that we might sell at the sign of the Star. Can you not manage to be captured by pirates, and enslaved in North Africa?"

There was a moment of stillness that was as sharp as a barber's blade. Then he let go my hand and smiled, though his eyes were grave under their flaxen brows. I had never before noticed the hue of them, but now I saw that they were gray, gray with a promise of blue.

"I will do my best," he said, "but the chances are not great."

"It was a jest," I said faintly.

"Our vessel has two hundred tons, two decks, and sixteen guns."

At first I thought he mocked me, but then I saw that he recited these things to calm his own fears, and I was sorrier than ever for my words.

"I should not have—"

"Farewell, Meg. Look after Anne, if you will."

"Of course. *Bon voyage*, Edward. I'm so glad for you."

But he was gone.

Whether by art or instinct, Will knew the moment I was alone, and came to sit again near the fire. I looked at him fearfully, wondering if he had heard my words to Anne's brother.

"Well," he said, sounding both amused and curious, "are you betrothed?"

Suddenly I was angry, and didn't want to wrestle with myself to keep my tongue quiet. "What are you talking of, you great dolt! Edward is an apprentice; he cannot marry until his term is served. He is as likely to be courting me as you are!"

He raised his eyebrows at that, then bent over the pages of manuscript on his knees. And at last I was given peace enough to read the story that had been so interesting to me at breakfast.

Two

~ I ~

I was uneasy the next day, in part because I knew I had been rude to Edward, but also because I didn't know how Anne would feel when she learned I had not received her brother's attentions kindly. I thought I would send her a little note of explanation, and then I thought I would not, and when my delay had turned from a few hours into three days she came to Little Britain Street late in the morning, and found me readying the pewter plates to be polished. I had already rubbed out the spots with salt and vinegar, and spread a paste of vinegar and chalk upon them, and I was just laying them in the sunlight that came through the south window when Deb brought Anne into the kitchen.

I believe it was the first time since the day we met that I wasn't glad to see her, and I knew she saw it in my face. Usually she was a cheerful girl, but she had a sober look as she asked me to walk with her to the Three Bells and dine there with her parents.

"I don't know if Susannah can spare me," I said without much hope, but when I asked, she spared me all too easily, and soon Anne and I were abroad. In the few days since Edward had sailed the weather had become mild, and something in the air gave me a restless, yearning feeling that made me wish my station in life were higher, or even lower, or that I had been foreign-born, or worshipped secretly like the Papists, or that I were bound on a long sea voyage to almost anywhere.

"Well, tell me what has passed," Anne said gravely as we walked. "Something has gone wrong, I see. Was it your father? Was he angry that Edward didn't speak first to him? 'Twas not Edward's fault, you know; I told him to speak only to you. Your opinions are so strong that I thought it best. Was I wrong?"

I wanted to tell her that she was very wrong; indeed, I had not known that a girl as sensible as Anne could be wrong so many times in one speech. But that did not seem a good way to begin. "My father wasn't there," I said instead. "My father doesn't know—does your own? Do all your family know that Edward came to see me on such business?"

She understood at once why I asked, and I saw her purse her lips before she opened them to speak. "You were not kind to him. He does not please you."

"I did not say so," I said, but my voice sounded guilty even to my own ears.

"Shoo!" Anne said angrily to a pig that rooted in the leavings that edged the road. And to me, in a voice that was more cold than angry, "They don't know. Indeed, he would not have spoken if not for my urging. I thought it such a chance for you. I didn't suppose that you could be foolish enough to turn away so fine a husband as Edward will make. He is my father's heir, you know."

"I don't care if he is the King's heir. I'm not so poor and plain that my friends must beg their brothers to woo me!" I replied angrily.

Anne's father was a vintner who imported wine from many countries and sold it to many taverns. He had a warehouse down by the docks, and a tavern in Cheapside, toward which Anne and I were now bound. The Gosse family had also a house in Broad Street, much larger and finer than ours: the wall hangings in the parlor were of silk and satin; and the candlesticks were nearly all of silver. I had been there many times, and always enjoyed myself among Anne's large, merry family. But her words stung, for I knew that her dowry was smaller than mine. Her family were too numerous, and lived too well, to provide her with a larger one.

"Hush, you misunderstand me," Anne said. She glanced at me, and then looked away. A coach went by, its wheels like thunder against the cobbles. When it had passed she said, "He thought he ought not to speak yet, because you are both so young, that is all. But it seemed to me that, as he was going away, and you worry so about your future—I thought he would do well to tell you of his feelings, that it would bring relief to you both. I'm sorry to have been wrong."

She looked more vexed than sorry, however, and I could not think how to mollify her. At last I said, "I do not know if I will ever marry. Perhaps I will keep house for Toby, and help him in the shop when he is grown."

She stopped in the street, and stared at me as if I had said I would pick pockets to get my living. "That is a thoughtless remark, even for you," she said seriously. "How could you choose never to command your own household, never to hire your own servants, never even to have the power of saying, 'Today we shall have mutton for dinner'? You would owe your obedience always to your father, or to your brother—or to your brother's wife." She shook her head. "Of all the girls I know, Meg, you are the least suited to stay single all your life!"

"If I married I would be under the command of my husband," I pointed out.

"That is different. To the right man you will be a partner, a helpmeet. That is why your choice of a husband is so important."

We had been standing before a coach yard in Foster Lane, and now from there came the sound of a hammer as it rang against an iron wheel, so we began to walk again.

"How can you speak in favor of marriage, when it is only a contest between a man and a woman to see who will be the first to cheat?" I asked her.

"Fie, Meg. You are looking to the playhouse for your answers, and not to life. Is there such a contest between your father and his wife? There is none between my parents, I promise you."

"I have seen such contests, and not at the playhouse," I said, thinking of some of the married pairs I knew, who sat together with their heads bowed at church on Sunday, and the rest of the week flirted and dallied with others.

Anne shrugged. "Too many couples have been brought together for money, and not for love."

I thought it strange in her to say this. "What of your own marriage, then? You don't mean that you love Mr. Rushworth?"

Mr. Rushworth was Anne's betrothed. I confess that he was not a favorite with me, for I thought him too fussy about little things and too lax about great ones. Besides, he was thirty-eight years old and his teeth were more than usually brown. However, I had heard Susannah say that Anne had made the best match that she could, and I did not doubt it, for her face was pitted from the smallpox.

She reddened at my question. "I have almost grown to love him," she said. "I will love him very soon. With every kiss I am closer."

"What! Do you give him kisses?"

"Why, yes, and—well, the papers are all signed, you know. But the important thing is that we are well suited. Of course, it is also a prudent match for me. I say nothing against prudence—only against greed. And you know it is not from greed that Edward wooed you."

"No, my dowry is hardly fine enough for that." I would have liked to ask her why he *did* woo me, for I had wondered mightily. Did he think me pretty? Did he admire me because I read widely, or because I could take down sermons in shorthand? Or—strange thought—could it be that he liked what my father called my impertinence? Though learned clerics have written much on the value of women's meekness, it has always seemed to me that plenty of men are happiest when henpecked. Was Edward such a man?

But I did not dare to ask his sister those questions. Instead I said, "Perhaps matrimony is a pleasing state for someone like yourself, Anne. You are nearly as skilled in the kitchen as my stepmother, and better with a needle than anyone I have ever met. But think of the biscuits I burn and the crooked seams I sew. If I marry, my life will be an endless round of tasks that I do poorly. It would be cruel in me to marry anyone I like so well as your brother."

She smiled in spite of herself, and then hid it while she said very soberly, "You know you are foolish. Leaving aside the great hurt you have given Edward, only think what you are saying. If things go ill you could easily end up in service, and there you might be commanded and abused by a master with as much power over you as the worst husband, a master with much less tolerance for burnt biscuits than my brother. Think of that!"

I did not want to think of that. I had thought of it many times. I knew well that marriage was the only prudent course for me, and that it had better come sooner rather than later. And yet when Edward shone his tenderness upon me like a lantern, I threw a jest at him to dim the glow. If a husband, why not Edward? He was a quiet, curious youth, interested in everything under the sun, seemingly, and more apt to ask questions than to give answers. Anne had told me once that his schemes for the improvement of her father's business were always taken up eagerly, because they were so clever. And as he was the oldest son, his prospects were secure.

We had reached our destination. The Three Bells was not large, having only eight hearths, but it was situated above the fine shops of Cheapside, and so was always busy. It was Mrs. Gosse who kept the tavern, greeting customers from behind the bar, dispatching servants to the cookshop next door for a plate of mutton or a hash of rabbit and lamb, and sending the potboy into the inner rooms with flagons of wine.

"Welcome, Meg!" she cried as soon as I stepped into the smoky tavern. "You are just in time for dinner! Mr. Gosse has already come from the warehouse, he is in the next room, and Henry is with him. I will be there directly." And she waved us on as she turned to give an order to the apprentice who drew the wine.

"Ah, here is the maid who wishes to study Latin and Greek," Mr. Gosse said when we entered the room where he sat with Anne's brother Henry. "And then what, Meg? For that would not satisfy you, hey? Then you would wish for mathematics, I'll wager, and astrology."

"And apothecary," Henry said, for he had lately been apprenticed to a man of that occupation, and would soon be learning to make medicines.

"That is not what I said," I protested. "I am perfectly satisfied with my own education. I only think—"

"They are jesting with you," Mrs. Gosse said as she joined us. "Pay no heed."

"No, do not mind me," Mr. Gosse said happily. "Instead, try this excellent sherry just in from the Canaries, and bought for a very good price—it is excellent, is it not, my dear?" he said to his wife.

"Nay, I had expected better," she said, in such a firm voice that I knew she would never change her mind.

"You are right my dear, it is not what it should be, but it is not bad—not bad at all," he replied, and poured a mouthful into my cup.

Then our dinner arrived, and we ate heartily, and when we finished, more wine was brought, and we drank healths to the King and to each other. We sampled several vintages, and Mr. Gosse thought each one fine—or said he did. After all, he was a merchant. But Mrs. Gosse continued to shake her head and say the sherry wasn't what it should be.

"What is ever as it should be?" Henry said. "You are too much like Edward, Mother."

"Or he is too much like me," she said with a smile.

"To Edward! May his journey bring him great good fortune, and may he return safely home to those who love him," cried Mr. Gosse, and we raised our glasses again.

It was a pleasant dinner, and I rose at last with reluctance, and only because I knew I was needed at the sign of the Star. I thought to myself that it would not be so hard a fate to be part of Anne's family.

"Don't be troubled," Anne whispered as she kissed me goodbye at the door. "Edward was right, that is all, you are both too young for such talk. We will not speak of it again for now."

But as I looked over her shoulder, I saw Mrs. Gosse taking her place behind the bar, and remembered that if I one day married Edward, that would be my place, as well. His world was made not of politics and plays but of tariffs and wine barrels. The thought made me quail. No, I could not bear such a life, after all. Better to stay unmarried, and take my chances on happiness, as we all must do.

2

And so I did not think again of Edward after I returned to the sign of the Star. Instead I thought of Will, to whom my father had given the work I wanted to do. He seemed much distracted of late, and I did not see him once with the pages my father had given him. Whenever there were no patrons in the shop he began a conversation with me, speaking of the Court, or the playhouse, or the Exchange; it hardly seemed to matter to him what we said. At last I could not bottle my curiosity longer, and asked him what had become of the account of Lord Stafford's execution.

"Why do you ask me that?" he demanded.

"Only that I am curious to know if you have mended it."

"It is not a task that can be done in a day."

"I did not say it was."

"I have been pondering it."

"Then you have read it, at least?"

"Of course I have read it. How can I mend it before I have read it?"

I said no more that day, for I had seldom known him to be so churlish, and I saw that I had touched a tender place.

The next day he did not start conversations with me, but kept a sheaf of papers before him as he stood behind the counter, and made careful notes upon a blank page with a quill. I had vowed to myself that I would not begin the subject again, and kept myself busy wiping the soot from the chairs and polishing the brass spittoon. But when he made a little noise of vexation with his tongue, I broke my vow almost before I knew I was doing so.

"Will it be the first thing you write?" I asked.

He spoke without lifting his head. "How could it be, when I'm nearly twenty-two? When I was at school I wrote essays on Christian virtue, the Roman Empire, Shakespeare's plays, and a dozen other subjects my masters chose for me. And I write my parents in Bristol every week."

"That is not the same."

"How is it different? The identical alphabet is used."

"Your parents will read your letters whether they are dull or not, but the man who picks up this story of Lord Stafford in the shop will put it down again without buying if you do not hold his interest."

Now he stopped his work and looked at me. "It is kind

of you to explain the nature of our business. I will do my best, if you will attend to your duties and allow me to work in peace."

I thought this unfair, for he had interrupted my reading many times in the past few days and I had not protested. But I was consoled by the words *I will do my best*. From a man as vain as Will it was nearly a promise of failure. Perhaps when my father had seen that his apprentice could not help him, he would give me the manuscript at last.

It was but a day or two later that I was asked to mind the shop alone, while my father met with one of his authors and Will was at the printer. The moment there were no customers to attend I began hunting for Mr. Phillips's manuscript, and at length I found it, though Will had folded the pages and hidden them between books, which he would not have done if he had not meant to conceal them. For a moment this gave me pause, and I wondered whether I was right in what I did. But I could not see how I harmed him merely by reading words upon a page. I read as quickly as I could, though it was difficult to keep my attention fixed when I was offered nothing but the dullest preaching and the most tedious details. I would not have believed that any writer could relate the story of an execution without some little moment of drama, but somehow Mr. Phillips had managed. Behind the manuscript itself were two pages of notes that Will had written, which ably laid

out the problems of the narrative, but offered no sugges-
tions for improving it. When I had finished reading I
folded the pages exactly as they had been before, and
tucked them carefully between the same two volumes.

Just then someone entered, which made me start, as
though he could have guessed that I was engaged in something secret. But when I saw that it was Mr. Winter I didn't
mind. Paul Winter was a faithful customer; we had been
acquainted many years. At one time he was too poor to buy
from us, but only paid a little money so that he might read
a book in the shop. In that way he spent many hours at the
sign of the Star, and we grew to know him well. Since then
he had inherited some land in Surrey from a cousin, and a
little capital with it; he had married well, and now bought
whatever books he liked.

We greeted one another warmly, and I asked him if he
had come for anything particular.

"Anything that is not about this supposed plot by the
Catholics!" he said. "I have read more than I care to already
about that sorry business."

I laughed. "Then you will not like our next. I believe
my father will publish an account of Lord Stafford's trial
and execution."

"An account that vindicates him?"

I opened my mouth to say that it didn't, and then
caught myself. "That I cannot say."

Mr. Winter shook his head. "It is easy to vilify a man in
these times—even a viscount, like Lord Stafford. I don't be-

lieve there was ever any plot to kill the King. It is just an easy way to persecute a man because his faith is strange to us."

"Very strange, for Papists are sworn to obey the Pope who lives in Rome, instead of their own King."

"We will not argue about religion. Tell me instead what you are writing?" For he was one of the few who knew about my scribbling; indeed, he had been the very first ever to learn of it, and had encouraged me in my avocation.

"I have been writing a story about a nobleman's daughter who travels with her father to Venice, and there discovers intrigues against the fortunes of her family," I said.

"Ah, Venice."

"Have you been there?"

"I have not had that pleasure."

"I wish that those of my sex could travel as freely as men," I said, thinking of Edward.

"Not every man travels freely. I have never been farther than Dover."

"But do you not long to sail the seas? To see the streets of Paris, or the Norwegian forests, or the canals of Venice?"

"My concerns lie here in England. But if you are so eager to travel, you may find the means. Perhaps you will marry a merchant."

Once again the conversation had come round to marriage. I wondered whether a maid could ever hope to discuss any other subject. "Of late I have not had the heart to write," I confessed to him. "I asked my father if I might help him with the account of Lord Stafford's execution, which he says needs much revision. But he will not hear of it. He gave it to Mr. Barlow to do instead."

"To Mr. Barlow," he repeated thoughtfully. "I see."

"I know that I could do it better. Will Barlow has never written anything more difficult than a letter to his family."

"Of course, your father is bound by contract to teach Mr. Barlow the business."

"That is not why."

"Why, then? Has he read your work?"

"He will not. He judges me by the titles I bestow upon my stories."

"He does not admire French heroic romances," Mr. Winter suggested.

"I don't write heroic romances. My tales are set in the present day."

"But you are much influenced by Mademoiselle de Scudéry, are you not?"

"What better influence can there be?" I retorted. I was uneasy and a trifle vexed, as though he accused me of something. "She writes skillfully on the subject of love, and she is never bawdy. She shows us the ideal to which we should aspire, and argues that our passions must always be governed by reason."

"You will certainly take no harm from reading her romances," Mr. Winter said with a broad smile. "I admit I'm more inclined myself to essays and poetry, but surely the world would be dull if all books were of a kind. You read things of all sorts yourself, or you once did—do you still?"

"Perhaps not of *every* sort. I have had as much advice for ladies as I can stomach, I confess."

Now he laughed out loud. "I think young people grow averse to books of advice just when they need them most." Then at last he began to search among the merchandise for something to take home with him. In time he chose a volume of philosophy by Niccolò Machiavelli, which we had lately reprinted. " 'Tis a pity your father does not read your work," he said as he put his coins upon the counter. "I think that he would be surprised at your skill. And someday you may choose to write in another form that he likes better."

"Perhaps it will be so."

"I am not a prognosticator, but I would not mind wagering a crown or two that your work will one day be in print. And when it is, I will buy the very first copy sold. You must be sure to tell me when you will be published; do you promise, madame?"

I laughed, and promised, and was much cheered by his faith in me.

~ 3 ~

Shortly after Easter, Anne married Ralph Rushworth. The wedding feast was large and lively, and two bride pies were served. One released larks into the room when cut open, and they sailed over our heads as we ate and danced, and another pie when opened showed a live snake curled within, instead of meat. It was great fun. After the feast was over, we all trooped together to Mr. Rushworth's lodgings to put the bride and groom to bed, and in the morning we stood under their window with a piper and a fiddler and roused them from their sleep. Then Anne and her husband went into the country for a few days, and when they came back I paid my first call on Mrs. Rushworth.

The lodgings Anne now shared with her husband were in Salisbury Court, near to Fleet Street. The girl let me in, but Anne sent her out at once to the Cheapside Market to shop for dinner. Then she showed me her rooms, which did not take a minute—there were but five. However, Anne had made them very pretty. Every corner had a little of her needlework in it. Much of it I had seen before, in Broad Street, but the bed curtains were entirely new, and bore great blooms of gold and coral and scarlet; indeed, they were nearly bright enough to drive the dark away.

"Now you are more qualified to argue for the married state," I said to her when we had settled in her parlor.

"There is nothing better," she answered, but I could tell that she lied. Anne's smile had always been so wide and merry that it drew all eyes to it in spite of her pitted face. But today it was small and thin, and I saw that she was unhappy.

"What is wrong, Anne?" I asked with my voice low, as though her husband were at home, instead of at the office where he clerked.

"Nothing. Nothing is amiss. It is just that he is more

particular than he seemed to be when he was courting me.
But that will pass—it is only that he is unsure of my skills,
because I'm so young. When I show him that I can manage
his household he will be content."

"He is unsure of *your* skills?" I asked in dismay, for if
Anne could be found wanting, it boded ill for any venture
I might make into marriage.

"Or else he is used to things another way, the way his
first wife made them. That is all, I know it. I will learn in
time how to please him."

"When you have a child you will not care what he
thinks," I said, seeking to cheer her.

"Fie, Meg, do you *never* grow up? You know we must
always strive to please our husbands."

I did not think this a great argument for matrimony,
but I dared not voice my thought with Anne in such a
mood.

As though she knew my mind she forced a smile and
said, "I have had a letter from Edward. He has reached
Leghorn."

"I'm so glad!"

"Yes, it is a great relief to know he has arrived safely.
The letter came only last night. Shall I read it to you?"

"I need not hear it all. Just tell me his news, unless you
yourself want especially to read it over."

"How clever you are to guess my feelings! That is just
what I would like."

And I saw that there was no way I could deny her the
pleasure of making me uncomfortable.

His writing was clear and careful, though no one would have called it lively. He described the ship he had sailed on, and I heard once more her tonnage, decks, and guns; and then he wrote of the passage to the Mediterranean, what good sail they had made, and how swiftly they had reached their destination. He spoke of the romance I had sold him, adding:

> *I am glad the cruel Moors no longer rule Spain, but I am troubled to see so many of them are now enslaved in Europe. Just yesterday I was offered an Arab slave at a good price; he was an old man but still of much usefulness. However, I remembered the Christians who are held captive in Muslim lands, and did not buy. There is a* Morisco *here, that is, a Spanish Moor, who will instruct me in Arabic, indeed, I have already begun my lessons, and can tell you it is no easy tongue.*

I thought to myself that if I had been he I would have bought the slave and treated him kindly, and freed him before returning to England. It seemed to me there would be something noble in such a deed. But perhaps it would not have been prudent. If the cost of buying a slave were spread over two years, would it be more or less than the cost of paying a servant? Either must be fed and housed . . .

It was the sound of my own name that drew me back. As I listened, Anne read:

Before I saw her I thought it did not matter if I received no encouragement, as we are both young, and I am likely to have many chances before me to earn her favor. But when I saw how very unwelcome my courtship was to her, I felt that it would be wrong to press her. She is a maid who knows her own mind. So I have resolved that I will think no more of marriage until my apprenticeship is served, and then I will ask my father to recommend to me a girl who is prudent and useful. Do not be disappointed, dear Anne, for I have resigned myself, and am quite cheerful, and grateful for my opportunities here. Not every marriage can be a love match, as you well know.

Anne lowered the page to her lap and looked at me gravely. "You didn't tell me your words to him were so very strong."

I had not let myself think of those words for many days, but as I recalled them now, my face flooded with heat. "I do not think they were *strong*," I said.

She looked at me doubtfully. "Perhaps he failed to understand you?"

"They were ill considered," I allowed.

"Why, what answer did you make?"

I could not bring myself to tell Anne that I had thoughtlessly wished ill upon her brother. "I—I made a jest."

"Oh, Meg! Poor Edward." But at last I saw the smile I

had been missing. "I shall write your excuses to him," she said.

I almost let this pass, for I regretted the hurt I had given him, and wanted to make it less. Yet I did not wish to give him hope where there was none. "I have already begged his pardon," I said. "I do not think anything more can be said on my behalf."

She looked at me searchingly for a moment, and saw in my face what I did not say aloud. Then she sighed. "I will not meddle, then," she said. "But, oh, Meg, you will be so sorry one day!"

I was despondent as I took my leave, for it seemed now that my thoughts about Mr. Rushworth had proved true, which meant that Anne would have no easy life before her. Besides that, hearing Edward's letter had made me gloomy. All the way home I pondered his words. *Not every marriage can be a love match.* Did he mean, then, that he loved me? I could not help but be pleased by the thought, yet at the same time I doubted; I did not see how it could be so. We had hardly seen each other over the past year, for he lodged with Mr. Nicholson, his master. Had he fallen in love with me while I argued with his father at table, or while we danced the courante? Did he love me merely because we laughed together for the space of a few hours? Had no maid ever laughed with him before? What special thing happens within a young man's heart that makes him declare to himself—and to his sister—that he is in love? I found it most perplexing. But in Edward's case it seemed to have been only a passing fancy, that he had now got over, and I felt disconsolate at the thought. *A maid who knows her own mind.* Of whom could he be speaking? Certainly no one could be so unsure of her own mind as I, for one moment I did not want ever to marry, and the next I was disappointed that Edward would not come courting anymore.

⤜ 4 ⤛

Of course I did not say to anyone that Anne and her husband had begun their married life unhappily, but I knew that she needed my friendship now more than she ever had, and for that reason I asked Susannah at supper one evening if I could make another visit to Salisbury Court the next morning, instead of helping Betty and Deb to scrub the staircases. My father was not at home that day, so only Susannah, Deb, Will, and I were at table, and we had eaten our hash very quickly.

"Certainly not," Susannah said in answer to my question. "Are you are becoming giddy, Meg? You are always running about the Town! I know not what young man you are trying to be near, but he will only think you idle if he sees you so often."

I could feel the angry blush upon my face, and stared into my plate, for I did not dare to look at Will to see if he was listening. It was hard to be called giddy when I sought only to bring comfort to an anxious friend, and the injustice of it rankled the more because I had been rebuked before Will.

After that I watched for a chance to speak with Susannah alone, and at last I found her in the parlor one evening after the little ones had gone to bed, stitching a length of bobbin lace onto the collar of a tiny linen shirt she was making for her unborn child.

"Shall I help you?" I asked, for I knew that a little service always smoothed the way where Susannah was concerned.

She looked surprised, and also doubtful. I guessed she did not trust me even to sew the tailclouts the new infant would need. But at last she pulled a torn nightshirt of my father's from a pile of mending, and I looked into her workbasket for a needle and thread. I drew my chair close to the wall, where a branch of candles was affixed, so that I might better see what I did. For a few minutes we worked in silence but for the pop and sputter of the fire. I did not want to speak amiss, or be abrupt, as I so often was, so I waited for Susannah to say the first word, and at last she did.

"I'm glad to see you at such work," she said. "For I worry about you, Margaret, and what will become of you when you marry."

"I am not in a hurry for that day," I said, but I looked without meaning to at the way her apron curved about her growing belly.

"I know that you are not. Yet it is well to be prepared. You do not know when someone may come courting."

"As my father came to you?"

She paused in her work, and looked at me, to try to judge my mood. It was an uneasy subject between us, for I had not wanted my father to remarry, and many months had passed before my stepmother earned my trust. I had never before asked her about my father's courtship.

"Did he speak to you first?" I asked. "Or was it to your father that he spoke?"

Her needle began to move again, and her eyes returned to her work. "My father had a letter, not from Miles himself, but from a cousin of mine, who knew him well. He wrote to describe your father's virtues—and his interest."

"And had you seen him then?"

"Not then, no. But my father liked the sound of him. I was not so sure, myself, because he was a widower—"

"With a daughter, too."

She glanced at me. "As you say. On the other hand, there was this advantage, that there was no son. So I agreed to a meeting. And there your father impressed me mightily." She smiled so, she looked almost silly. "How could it have been otherwise? For he is a man of sense and probity, and"—she smiled—"he is a well-looking man."

I considered this information with surprise. I had never before thought of how my father might appear to women.

"And you did not think him too old?"

"It is best that a husband have greater experience, that he might guide his wife in their life together. And his business was well established."

"And it is the *book* business," I said. "Did that count with you?"

"Nay, not as it does with you," Susannah said, smiling as she sewed. "Your father might have been a grocer or a goldsmith, it would not have mattered. It is himself I love, and not his business. But you—*you* are in love with printed pages. I have told your father to discourage all who do not belong to the Stationers' Company."

I could not tell if she was teasing me or if she had truly said such a thing to my father, but I did not like to ask. Instead I said, thinking of Anne, "But how did you know that you would like him . . . afterward?"

"Why, I asked many, many questions, or my mother did. I listened to gossip. I tried to discover if your mother had had her own dress allowance, and whether she had been seen with blacked eyes. I looked at you when I came to the shop—"

"At *me?*"

"—to see how you were treated. In the end I was satisfied, and, thank the Lord, I was not wrong."

I had come to the end of the rent I had been mending. The cloth did not quite match up on either side of it. I peered at my work, wondering how it was that I could not get even such a simple thing right. I imagined my future husband asking sly questions about the state of my workbasket, and suddenly I found I had dropped a large, hot tear upon my father's nightshirt.

"Do not be afraid," Susannah said gently. "You will

have much help in making your choice, help from those who are wiser than you. And I promise you will enjoy courtship! I think there is no finer time for a maid than this, when she is not quite won and must be wooed."

"You do not speak to me, *now*, as if I were a flirt or a flibbertigibbet, who runs all over Town to be near the man she admires," I said.

"Ah, Meg, did I displease you when I said so? It was a careless speech. I didn't mean it."

"But we were not alone. My reputation . . ." I could not finish.

"Why, who was there? Only Deb and Will. Do not trouble yourself, Meg, Will knows that you are no flirt."

I didn't care two straws whether Will thought me a flirt or not. But I wanted to be treated with respect when he was by, as though I were as valued in the household as he was himself.

～ 5 ～

Not long after that, Anne and I went one afternoon to the playhouse at Dorset Gardens to see the second part of *The Rover*, which was by Aphra Behn. It was a clever comedy, set in Italy at Carnival time and full of such intrigues and mistakes as happen more often upon a stage than in life. Afterward I walked with Anne back to Salisbury Court, and from there made my way home, thinking all the time about the widow Mrs. Behn. She was the only

Englishwoman I had ever heard of who earned her living by her pen. I wished I might do the same, but I wasn't sure I had enough of ability and luck to be the second such woman, and I did not think I was made to bear the poverty that I saw among the playwrights who came to Little Britain Street. Few were as comfortable as Mr. Dryden.

When I entered the shop I saw Will behind the counter, with pages before him and his quill in his hand, while my father stood nearby fastening his coat.

"How fortunate that you have come, Daughter," he said when he caught sight of me. "I had wanted to take Will with me to the coffeehouse. Now you can mind the shop while we go. It will be closing time very soon, in any case," he added, glancing at the window to judge the light.

Will gathered his pages hastily together and put them beneath the counter—he had not time to do more. I almost pitied him, for I thought I could guess his feelings as he followed my father into the street.

As soon as they had gone, I retrieved the papers and began to read by the fading daylight. Almost at once I felt triumphant, for though he had taken out the dreary preaching, the paragraphs were still long and dull, with no word that enticed or entertained. But as I read on, I grew interested in spite of myself, and began to fret that he had done some things well, though not all.

I was nearly to the end when Will rushed into the shop.

"What is wrong? Where is my father?" I asked with surprise.

"At the coffeehouse. He sent me for his pipe." He stood

there panting, so that I knew he had run through the streets. The black curls of his wig were disordered, and for once his mouth did not mock.

"It is there, upon the mantel," I said.

He didn't turn. "You are reading my work."

"There were no customers."

"It is not finished," he said. He looked away from me. "It is not well done."

It was the sort of moment I dreamed of when I was angry at him for his arrogant ways. But I have noticed that the moment anyone confesses weakness to me, my anger fades, and I am concerned only to make that person feel better. It is my own weakness, I suppose.

"It is done much more ably than Mr. Phillips did it," I offered.

"But it is so dull at the start."

Later I was angry at myself, and wondered why I acted as I did. But at the time I didn't pause. "That is because you have begun in the wrong place. Bishop Huet writes that a history must begin in the middle of the story, so as to give some suspense to the reader."

"Who is Bishop Huet?"

"He wrote *A Treatise on Romances and Their Originals*. Mademoiselle de Scudéry always starts her stories in that way. You must begin at the block, with the crowd waiting to see the axe fall. Then you may tell how he came there."

"But romances are only stories. This is the truth."

I shrugged. "The truth will not be any less true for being told in a different order. Besides, how do you know it is the truth? The longer the road, the greater the chance that part of what you carry will be dropped along the way. Between the executioner's block and Mr. Phillips's pen there was a great distance, and between Mr. Phillips's pen and yours there is another distance. Much of the truth has already been dropped."

"I shall not model my work on that of a French story-teller," he said stubbornly.

I was relieved to hear it, for already I regretted my advice. But Will was no fool. Three days later my father came to dinner boasting of what a fine writer his apprentice was, and what a great publisher and bookseller he would be one day. And when the thing was printed, and I opened a copy that still smelt of ink, and looked upon page one, I saw that it began at the block.

I resolved that day that I would never again take pains to make Will Barlow feel better. All the same, I half admired him because he had not thrown away his chance—as I had done.

Three

☙ I ❧

Look there," Will said to me one Tuesday early in May.
"That is the fifth man that has stopped at Mr. Taylor's
stall in the past quarter hour. I wonder what new thing he
is selling."

We were in St. Paul's Churchyard, where my father had
rented a stall for a few days, as he did from time to time
when he wished to add to the earnings of his business. The
skies were low and gray that afternoon, and the wind was
high; many people hurried by, but few paused—except at
Mr. Taylor's stall.

"I will find out," I said to Will, and before he could argue with me I had crossed the street.

I smiled at Isaac Biddle, Mr. Taylor's apprentice. "Will
and I have made a wager," I said to him. "He says you are
drawing so many customers because you are selling your

books at half their price; but I say you are selling something very bawdy. Which of us is right?"

"Neither, but you are closer," he said.

He held up a small, stitched book, and I read its title: *A True Account of the Trial of John Francis Dickison, Popish Priest, Who Persuaded Martha Cook to Renounce Her Protestant Religion, for Which He Was Sentenced to Be Drawn and Quartered.*

Now I wished I had not asked. Will would not like to learn that this pamphlet sold so well when his own account of Lord Stafford's execution had not, though my father said it was only because we had published it so long after the viscount's death that the public had lost interest.

Just then two men paused near me, and I moved a little, that I might not hinder them from looking over the merchandise.

"Where do you want to dine?" one man said to the other as he took out his purse.

"Why not the Three Bells?" the other man said.

I hardly listened—I was thinking of what I might say to Will.

"The Three Bells will be closed, have you not heard? Philip Gosse died last night."

The shock of it was so great that I gave a little cry, like a cat whose tail has been stepped upon, and both men turned to stare at me.

Will had been watching me closely, and saw that something was wrong. "Meg, what is it?" he called.

I turned and went back to our stall. "Anne's father. The man said—he said that Anne's father has died. It cannot be true, can it? I would have had a note from Anne."

"We left very early," Will said. "You had better go to Broad Street and find out."

So I went, hoping to find it was a false report. But the rumor proved true; Anne's father had died, and the Gosse house was filled with disorder, anxiety, and grief.

Now I did not need to beg my stepmother for hours to spend with Anne; indeed, sometimes Susannah and I went together to the house on Broad Street, for there was much to be done to settle the estate, and there was also the business to be attended to. Mrs. Gosse took over the running of the warehouse, and Anne kept the Three Bells, though Mr. Rushworth did not want her to do it, and they had a fierce quarrel. At last he agreed that she might work only until Edward came home. Word had been sent at once to Leghorn, but it would take weeks for the letter to reach him, and weeks for a ship to bring him back to England.

In the meantime, there was the funeral to be arranged: a hall to be rented and draped in black, mourners to be hired. A richly embroidered pall of black velvet was borrowed from the Vintners' Company; it would be draped over the coffin as it was carried through the streets. It fell to me to go to the printer for the tickets, which were adorned with skulls and skeletons; together Anne and I filled in the blank spaces with her father's name and the date, time, and place of the funeral.

Perhaps if Edward, who was not extravagant, had been

home, the funeral would not have been so grand. But that is not certain, for the greatness of it honored Philip Gosse, and Edward would have wanted that. Nearly three hundred came, though only a hundred and eighty had been sent tickets. White mourning gloves were given to the guests and even to the servants. For those who bore the pall—my father was one of these—there were hatbands of black crepe, and very fine mourning rings. Burnt claret was served, and sugar cakes and rolls and macaroons, and so many other biscuits that even the uninvited had their fill. When all had drunk and eaten, we were each of us given a sprig of rosemary to hold, and we made a procession through the night to the church. The paid mourners walked in pairs before the hearse—forty-six old men, one for each year of Philip Gosse's life. Then came the mourning coach, and twenty-nine coaches after it, all filled with City merchants and their families. So many wax torches were blazing that we lit the night as we traveled through it.

"I didn't know they were such a wealthy family," Will said as he looked out the window of the coach my father had rented for the occasion. "Think how much all those wax torches must cost. Whoever marries Edward Gosse will do well for herself."

I gave him a sharp look, but said nothing.

"You would do better to keep your mind on death and resurrection," Susannah observed.

My father made a sound that was part murmur and part grunt, and after that we fell silent, as though we feared to contradict the opinion he had thereby expressed.

At the church, the coffin was set upon trestles while we heard the sermon.

"Though his body lies without sense or motion, as though it were a block of stone," Reverend Little preached, "though all majesty and beauty has gone from the flesh, and it will soon putrefy and rot, we must not look upon it as a lost and perished carcass, for it has within a seed of eternity, and the hope of a glorious resurrection."

I kept my head lowered and tried to think of Anne's father made whole and new in paradise, but instead I beheld him lifting his tankard to drink the King's health, or raising the bow to his fiddle, and I wept.

In the churchyard we threw our sprigs of rosemary onto the coffin, and by torchlight watched the first earth fall upon it while Reverend Little intoned those same words that had been said over the coffin of my mother, and all my tiny sisters and brothers that lived such a little time: "Earth to earth, ashes to ashes, dust to dust; in sure and certain hope of the resurrection to eternal life."

Then the family and closest friends went back to Anne's house, which again was all in black, even to the bedding. There we drank the rest of the burnt claret while we told stories of beautiful deathbed prayers or reported the strange evidence we had heard of ghosts. We spoke consolingly to the anxious widow and her children, and to each other we spoke in low voices about the estate. Some thought it would prove to be small, because Philip Gosse had spent so freely while he lived; others believed that it would prove to be of surprising value.

"The business will be all in a tangle, for none of the children are old enough to inherit, and their portion must be put aside," said old Mrs. Snow with a doleful shake of her head.

A voice beside me said, "Edward will make everything right."

It was Anne's brother Peter who spoke. Today was the first time I'd seen him in more than a year, for he studied at Oxford, but he had come home for his father's funeral. He reminded me powerfully of his eldest brother, with the same fair hair that Edward had and something of the same air as well, at once awkward and confident.

Mrs. Snow did not at all mind being caught talking of the estate. "We'll see what is discovered at the appraisal," she said to Peter, and went to have her glass refilled.

"I'm sure the appraisal will go well," I said, wanting to give him comfort.

But he said, "When Edward comes home, *then* all will be well."

～ 2 ～

When wind and weather proved favorable it could take as little as two or three weeks for a ship to travel from Italy to England, but when the elements did not cooperate it might take two months, or even longer. Therefore no one was troubled as the weeks passed and nothing was heard of Edward Gosse; indeed, except when I was with Anne, who could talk of no other subject, I hardly thought of him at all.

It was in the third week of June, near to midsummer, that we at last had news.

The day was warm and fair. Though I could not feel the sun upon my face—the shop was well shaded against its rays so that our pages might not curl—I could at any rate see it shining upon the door knocker of the house opposite, as though something wonderful were inside, instead of old Mr. Foxworthy, who had lived there full seventy years.

"When I have my own shop, I will keep the accounts with double entries," Will said as he looked over the ledger.

"I have heard of that," I said, looking up from my book with interest. "But if you do not keep memorials in your ledger, you will have no record of which customers prefer which sorts of books."

"A good merchant will always remember that. But nothing is so dangerous to business as wrong accounts, and this method provides a check upon the figures, so that errors are quickly caught."

"Well, you may keep your books how you like, I suppose."

"I will do everything as I like, when I have my own shop," he said, putting down the ledger with the air of one who begins a favorite subject. "I will sell many books of advice—and especially books written for the edification of ladies, for they have leisure to read that not all men have."

I was too wary to answer this remark.

"And of course they are in great need of such edification, especially regarding morals, because of their weak understanding."

I persisted in my silence, triumphant that I had seen his tendency early enough to avoid a trap. But Will used many strategies.

"My wife will advise me regarding these books," he continued.

"Your wife! You had better be sure she knows no Latin."

"I am not likely ever to meet a woman who does," he replied.

At that I could not help smiling, thinking of the pleasure it gave me to look into a book of Cicero's speeches now and then, the way climbing over a fence into someone else's garden brings delight. I confess I never lingered long.

"I know why you smile," Will said.

I looked at him with surprise.

"Mr. Edward Gosse will soon be in London; that is what makes you happy."

"How soon he will be in London depends upon the wind and weather."

"No doubt he will come to the sign of the Star for something to read as soon as he is here."

"Straightening out his father's affairs will surely be his first business."

"He will find the time to come here, I wager. And I know just which book I shall recommend to him."

He waited for me to ask which, but I said nothing. I

did not like how Will so often forced a conversation this way or that, and robbed me of the freedom to choose my words.

"You could guess it if you chose," he continued without my encouragement. "I shall offer him *Mysteries of Love and Eloquence; or, the Arts of Wooing and Complementing.* It is just what he needs."

I could hardly keep from laughter. "That is the last book you could sell to a man like Mr. Gosse," I said, thinking of the Latin poetry Edward preferred for his courting. *Mysteries of Love and Eloquence* was full of bawdy verses, such as: *Ellen, all men commend thy eyes / Only I commend thy thighs.* And it gave advice on how men might tumble maids in private corners of London. And much more—I knew it all, for I had read every word of it.

"It will help him enormously," Will said. "It has certainly helped *me.*"

"You could not have had any success in wooing *without* help," I returned, and laughed with pleasure, for I seldom got the best of him.

Before he could retort, Anne came through the door of the shop in a billow of black mourning, and as she took down her hood I could see that something was very wrong.

"Anne! Why are you not at the tavern? What can be the matter?" I cried as I rushed to take her hand.

"It is Edward. He didn't wait for the convoy—he knew how urgently he was wanted here at home. He took the first ship bound for England, it had but three guns—"

I sickened as she spoke, knowing what she would say next.

"—and it fell to Algerine pirates!"

"God forgive me," I said.

Will and Anne looked at me strangely, for neither knew of my words to Edward before we parted. I almost told them at that moment, for I could not help wondering if by wishing this fate for him I had brought it to pass, and I longed for someone to tell me it was not so. Luckily, Will spoke before I could, and I had time to realize that it was Anne, and not myself, who stood in need of comfort.

"Do not be troubled, Mrs. Rushworth," Will soothed her. "The ransom can be sent at once, can it not?"

"It cannot!" Anne said with despair. "We lost many casks of Madeira in a shipwreck not long before my father's death, and then Mother had to settle my father's debts before the estate could be divided. And—and we spent so much on *mourning*." By now Will had guided her to one of the cane chairs, and she sank upon it, slapping at the skirt of her taffeta gown as she did so, as if to punish it for how much it cost.

I found my voice at last. "Then you have done rightly to come to us. We will see what help my father can give. Will, do you know where Mr. Moore is today?"

"He was to dine at the King's Head in Charing Cross. Shall I go for him?"

"At once, please."

"But shall I send for Deb first?"

"Nay, I will attend to Anne myself."

"But—but are *you* well, Meg?"

I looked at him in astonishment. "Go at once," I said again, and he obeyed me.

Anne hardly noticed his leaving. "The ransom is so very great. They can tell that he is not a sailor, so they guess that he is rich. But we are not rich, not as rich as that. Who knows how long he may be enslaved in Algiers?"

"Hush! Hush!" But though I could stop her speech, I could not stop my thoughts. By now he had been sold, by now beaten—how many blows, how many times? By now he was being made to wait upon others, or build their walls, or dig their pits. Or perhaps he lay in chains, gnawed by rats . . .

Anne had other horrors in mind.

"What if he should turn Turk?" she whispered.

"Hush, Anne, of course he will not," I said, yet I understood her fear. Many Englishmen who had been captured by Barbary pirates had chosen to free themselves by renouncing their Christian faith and swearing allegiance to the religion of Muhammad. After that, of course, it wasn't easy to come home. Most of them lived out their renegade lives in foreign places. Some became pirates themselves, or soldiers, and so took up arms against their own countrymen.

But Edward wasn't a common seaman, who might expect to wait years for his ransom to be paid.

"He has always been lax about his catechism," Anne said mournfully.

"Those who turn Turk have nothing in England to come back to that is better than the lives they can have in North Africa," I reminded her. "For Edward it is different."

She looked at me in a certain way, and I guessed she was thinking that she wished I had given him yet one more reason to come home.

My father soon came, and spoke with Anne; later he and Susannah went to see Mrs. Gosse. They consulted also with Susannah's father, and with Edward's master, Mr. Nicholson, and other City merchants. For nearly two weeks there was a kind of buzz about the Town, the kind produced by great activity when it is joined to great hope. But then the buzz slowed, fell, failed. It seemed that in spite of how greatly Edward was esteemed by his family and friends, by merchants and by other apprentices, by his neighbors and by the folk who sat in the pews near to his at St. Botolph—in spite of all this, the sum needed to ransom him simply could not be raised.

~ 3 ~

And then—everything went on as before. I could not make sense of this. It was as though Edward's capture were a sword that passed through our lives without cutting. Anne went on quarreling with Mr. Rushworth and working at the Three Bells in spite of what he said. Mrs. Gosse went on buying Muscadine and selling Mosel and bribing

customs officials. My father went on selling poetry and
plays, Susannah's belly went on swelling, Will went on giv
ing me orders and watching me like a cat as I fought my
temper. As for me, I clutched Toby to me over and over,
and said, "I'm sorry, I'm sorry," into his coats, as though he
were the only one with the power to forgive me for wishing
Edward into slavery.

"Are you *nearing* the amount needed?" I asked Anne
one Sunday after divine service. "Is it almost collected?"

Anne gave her head a quick shake, then looked around,
as though to shake one's head were treasonable. "I do not
think we even go in the right direction," she said in a low
voice. "I believe we have less than we had the day the news
first came. But I must be off, I open the Three Bells this afternoon."

"I will walk with you," I said, and we set out toward
Cheapside. "How can there be *less*?"

"Merchants who were willing to help that day are no
longer willing: men who said they would loan us money
now ask for more security than Mother can produce.
Everyone is afraid that the business will founder. Even Mr.
Rushworth—" She stopped herself.

"What has he to do with it?" I asked in surprise.

"I am the only one who has received my portion of the
estate, because I am married, you know. I begged Mr.
Rushworth to use it toward Edward's ransom, or even a
part of it, but he will not."

"He counts on it for his advancement, I suppose," I

said. "Soon he will have a large family to support!" I hoped with this to tease a smile from her, for she had spoken often of her desire for many children.

But she only sighed. "Ralph is angry with me because I work at the tavern," she said. "He stays out very late each night. Perhaps he takes his pleasure elsewhere."

"Most likely he is only at the alehouse," I said to console her, but she shook her head woefully. "Does the tavern do well?" I asked. "Will Edward's ransom come from there?"

"It does better than the warehouse," Anne allowed. "But Mother uses the profits to buy claret, because the price is good. She says she must save the business, or there will be nothing for Edward to come home to. My brother Henry has taken a leave from his apprenticeship with the apothecary, that he might help at the warehouse. We have released two of our own apprentices. My brother Peter has come back from Oxford—we can no longer afford the fees. And Father so wanted one of his children to go to university. Oh, if he had never died!"

By now we had reached Cheapside, and the stairway to the Three Bells. I hated to leave her in such gloom, but I could not feel comfortable in a tavern on a Sunday, so we said farewell, and I made my way back to Little Britain Street.

As the days passed, I tried to turn my thoughts from Edward's captivity, as others seemed to have done, but I could not. One afternoon in the shop I took up my quill and began to write what I could not banish from my mind. These were the words I set down:

> *The Englishman lay still, with his eyes closed. Above him two huge Turks spoke to each other in their own tongue, which makes every word sound like an angry curse. A rope descended, it flayed the Englishman's skin, and the blood flowed freely. But he did not cry out. "It is for Christ I suffer," he said, and his captors snarled like dogs. The rope landed again upon the man's back. His cheeks were pale with suffering.*

That was when Mr. Winter walked in.

"Good afternoon, madame! I'm glad to see you writing once more. What is it today?"

I put my hand upon the sheet, and took it up again, smeared with ink.

"You need not show me if you do not like," Mr. Winter said gently.

I lifted a corner of my apron and wiped my hand against it, feeling foolish.

"Perhaps when it is done," he suggested.

I shook my head. "It is nothing. Nothing. But I cannot drive it from my mind." Suddenly I thrust the page toward him, as though it were the water at Cana, and he were Our Lord, who could turn it to wine.

He took it up and read it quickly, but he did not turn it to wine. Instead he gave me a look I did not like. "Why do you write this?" he said, almost angrily. "What does it help?"

I didn't answer, but looked at him without understanding. I had not written it to help. I had written it because I must.

"Write something better," he said more softly. "Write something that *will* help."

Could anything help? I looked at him with fierce concentration. "A letter to the King?" I asked at last.

He shrugged. "If you like. Though he does not pay even what he owes to the poor sailors who have been so long in his service. I have always thought it is easier to get money from the poor than from the rich, and easiest to get it from those who are in between."

"A Charity Brief. To be read at all the parishes of London, seeking donations for the ransom."

"There! And you are the one to write it, I am sure."

Then he bade me look out some poems by Abraham Cowley, and I found them for him.

A Charity Brief. It must be issued by the King's Printer, of course, but that should not prove difficult. Such appeals came commonly enough, sometimes pleading for the relief of those who had suffered from fires or floods, and other times for this very cause, the redemption of Christian slaves from the Barbary Coast. Why had it not yet been tried on Edward's behalf? Because none of Edward's womenfolk could spare the hours, I supposed. But I could.

I took a new page and dipped my quill once more into the ink.

Four

What stirs the heart? I wondered as I worked on the Charity Brief. I wanted men and women to gasp when they heard it, I wanted tears to roll down their faces, but most of all, I wanted them to unclasp their purses. What would lead to that? Must I rouse fear, or remorse, or anger, or pity, or all at once? I spent every spare moment engaged in this task, even writing in Will's presence, which usually I did not do. I could not remember ever striving so to make each word the mightiest it could be.

"Do you write a letter to Mr. Gosse?" Will asked one day after several glances toward my work.

"I write what is more useful—a Charity Brief on his behalf."

He replied as though curious, "You will not give him up, though his family have."

"They have not! But they lack the time—and the

heart—for this work. Remember that they suffer under a double tragedy, which I do not feel in the same way."

He lifted his eyebrows, and the curls of his wig bobbed upon his forehead, but he said no more, and I was left to read over what I had written.

Redeem this man from slavery! His family are desperate for his return. His brothers and sisters depend upon his care, and I, his mother, am very lately widowed. The family business to which Edward Gosse is heir must founder if his speedy ransom be not obtained.

While we in London sit in our pews and hear these words proclaimed, what is passing with Mr. Gosse in Algiers? We do not know the particulars, but from what has befallen others in his situation we can guess that he labors beyond his strength, perhaps rowing a galley, or drawing a cart, as though he were a beast. He is doubtless hungry, yet can hardly stomach the foul scraps he is thrown; he is likely to be so thirsty that his dry tongue cannot utter sounds, yet his captors laugh when he gestures for water. Or worse—they beat him until he is nearly senseless; he endures so many blows upon his body that he cannot tell the source of his pain. And when the flesh is torn, his wounds are washed in salt and vinegar, so that his suffering might swell and grow, until it has swallowed up every other thing in life.

But that is not the worst. These tyrants who are

the professed enemies of Christ do more than abuse the body of a man in their power. They also revile his faith; they endanger his very soul by their daily assault upon it. Let every parishioner who hears this plea heed it well, every master and mistress, every lodger, every sojourner who but passes through. Give shillings if you have them, and if you have them not, then give your pennies, for upon your Christian charity hang the life and the eternal salvation of Edward Gosse.

Before I showed the Brief to my father, I took it to Mrs. Gosse, in whose name I had written it. I found her in the warehouse, a narrow, drafty building near the docks that smelled of wet wood and spilt wine. Some men were loading casks onto a cart, and Mrs. Gosse was frowning over her ledger at a table near the window, where only a little light came through the small squares of green glass. She looked as though even to hold her shoulders set made her weary, and it pained me to see her so.

When I came before her, she glanced up at me and said, "I told him we must start keeping the books with double entries. But he left it for another day, again and again."

"Yes, we are thinking of that at the Star, too," I said, before I remembered that it was Will who thought of it, and not my father.

"But you have not come about that." She closed the book. "What is it, Meg—does your father need some claret for his table?"

I almost wished I had come with an order for wine, and the shillings to pay for it, instead of a page that might bring nothing. Without speaking, I offered it to her. She took it and read it, slowly, holding it away from her face to see the characters more clearly.

Then she looked up at me. "If it could only bring him back!" she said. "Oh, Meg. I hardly dare to hope. For I do not know how long it will take to gather such a sum from the earnings of the business."

I pressed her hand. "I have your consent, then, to publish this in your name?"

"My consent and thanksgiving," she said. "But I do not know if it will be enough, unless the curates canvass the parishes. And who will persuade them to do that?"

"I will," I said.

I knew that I must next show it to my father, though to do so was not easy for me. They say a man is the head of his family the way the King is the head of his country. Perhaps that is why every word my father spoke carried so much power, and could make me sting, or fight, or fall, as though it were a weapon. Because it was so, I had to see him alone; I did not want to be rebuked in front of Will or Susannah. Therefore I waited up for him in the parlor until the early hours of the morning.

All my life he had been sparing with his words of praise, and yet I knew that once he had prized my quickness. Because there was no one else I cared so much to please, I had learned to read his pleasure in signs as small as a glance. But even his glance forgot me more often since Will had come to work in Little Britain Street.

"Why, Daughter," my father said in surprise when he came home at last. "It is late to find you sitting up. Is something amiss?"

I rose to greet him, but he gestured to me to take my chair again, and sat himself, so I answered him, "Nothing is amiss here at the Star, but much is amiss for the Gosse family."

"Aye, they have suffered two sore blows," my father agreed.

"I want to help them, Father."

He spread his hands, and the firelight glinted on the rings he wore on his fingers. "I have offered what I can spare toward Mr. Gosse's ransom."

"I have written a Charity Brief in his mother's name. She has seen it and given her consent. Will you take it to the King's Printer for her?" And I offered him the page.

He gave me a grave look before he took it, but I could not read its meaning. Then he took out his spectacles and read the appeal by the light of the fire. I could tell when his eyes had reached the bottom of the paper, but instead of lifting his gaze, he began again at the start and read it a second time. Then he took off his spectacles and looked at me as though he had not seen me in several years.

"It is boldly written," he said.

I thought he reproached me, because I was not modest as befits my sex, and it did not seem fair to me. "Must not such a plea be boldly written to gain its end?" I asked.

"Indeed. I believe that, of its kind, I have heard nothing more persuasive. There is a fire in it that I did not expect."

Gladness poured through me, and I sat very straight in the chair. "Then you will take it to the King's Printer?"

He did not answer, but sat looking down at the spectacles in his hand, tilting them so that the firelight flared and darkened in the glasses. Finally he looked at me again. "Why do you do this, Margaret?"

I could almost have answered, *To hear you say I write with fire,* but of course I did not. "I have told you, Father. To help the Gosse family."

"And for no other reason?"

"No, Father."

He made a little grunt of satisfaction. "I will take it to the King's Printer," he said.

"I have written on a serious subject in this Brief, have I not?"

"Indeed," my father replied.

"Now that I have shown you that I can do so"—already by this moment in my sentence I saw that his face was fixed in denial, but I did not falter—"may I be of help to you in preparing manuscripts for the printer?"

"Stop it, Margaret! Stop it!" I do not think his voice ever sounded harsher to my ears. "You said this Brief was written only for the sake of the Gosse family! Did you write it instead to display yourself? You must cease this folly, you must! You will become a laughingstock. Everyone but you sees how unfitting it is."

"I did not mean to tease—"

"I do not speak of teasing. I mean that you must stop this senseless scribbling you do at all hours. It begets nothing but laughter!"

"This—this—" I had to stop and begin again, to steady my voice. I held the page aloft, that he had said was writ with fire. "This will beget something beyond laughter," I said at last.

"Yes, yes, you may write such things if you will. It is very proper in a maid to do works of charity. But for the rest, I beg that you will stop at once."

I stared at the brass firedogs in the grate. "You do not— you do not *forbid* me to write?"

He, too, looked into the grate a moment, and then at me. "I forbid that any writing you do should come to the ears of others," he said at last. I lifted the page from my lap again, and he added, "Except this Brief."

I sat still and silent. I thought of how glad I had been only a few minutes before, to hear him admire my words.

"Do not sit there stricken!" he said angrily. "It is for your own good that I say this, that you may marry well. I do not ask that you give up reading books, or talking about them, or selling them. Marry into the trade, if you like. A woman may be a great helpmeet to a man in business, as your mother was to me. It is not such a bad fortune. But no woman will better her reputation by writing poetry and romances."

He said this last that I might argue with him. It was his way, when he had hurt me, to invite my argument. But it was just when he had hurt me that I could not raise my voice. "Who laughs at me?" I asked at last.

"No one laughs at you—*yet.*"

But I did not believe him.

Who laughs at me? I wondered for three days running, while I helped Betty scour the pots with sand, or lifted Toby into my arms, and each day I grew more angry. Was it Susannah who had put this thought into my father's head? I wanted to think so, but somehow I did not. Yet how many knew of my long labors with the quill? Anne knew. I had often made a present to her of a story or a set of verses. And indeed, she sometimes laughed at me, though never cruelly. But perhaps she had told others. Was it Mr. Rushworth who spoke of me with ridicule, in words that traveled on many tongues back to my father's ear? Surely it could not be Mr. Winter, who encouraged me so. I knew it was not he.

It might be *Will.* I could all too easily imagine him in conversation with my father, with his brows lifted and his mouth mocking. But did he know that I wrote? And would even Will despise me to my father's face?

Whoever it was, he would not stop my pen, not even for a day! I had seen the look in my father's eyes when he read my Brief, and I meant to see that look again, in his face and in other faces, too. I was determined that some-day my father would change his mind under the force of the pages I would fill. Or if he did not, I would publish in secret with one of his rivals, using a false name, and he would wish *he* had the copyright on the work that sold so well!

That was my resolve. But in truth I would not have shared what I wrote over the next week with anyone, even if my father had never said a word upon the subject. For, again and again, I wrote of Edward. I showed him in his captured vessel, firing the cannon when the gunner fell, then falling in his turn, his blood spilt upon the deck . . . I showed him bound in a cellar, gazing with horror upon a serpent that slithered toward him . . . I showed him laboring for his tyrannical master, weary almost beyond bearing, yet reaching to catch a fellow Christian as he swooned under the fierce Algerine sun . . . I showed him with his skin flayed, his cheeks hollowed, his spirit undaunted, his faith unflagging . . . I showed him trying courageously to escape, only to be caught, and flogged, and flogged again until at last he moved no more, and the flies settled upon the bloody stripes that painted his back . . .

With every word I wrote, my fears increased. And yet I could not keep myself from writing, the way a dog cannot keep from scratching at his fleas, even when to do so makes him bleed.

☙ 2 ❧

The Brief was read for the first time on a Sunday late in July, and the collection was good—or so I was told by one curate after another. But it was not nearly enough. And though I had pretended to myself that I expected little, the truth was that I expected much, and when it did not come to pass I blamed the Brief I had written, and did not think it fine after all, but weak and dull, and I felt ashamed. Then I was stern with myself, for I had not written the Brief to exhibit my skill but to win Edward's freedom.

I saw that I would have to visit the churches one by one, and urge the curates to go door to door in their parishes, if Edward was to be soon ransomed. To do this I would need time. I weighed in my mind if I was more easily spared from my morning duties to the household, or my afternoon duties to the business, and at last I resolved to speak to my father. It was not easy to find the right time, however, and for two days I put it off, each day thinking another day would be better.

Then one evening I was in the dining room, giving Toby his supper, when Will came to the sideboard and took up the flagon of wine there. "Well," he said with his mocking smile as he turned to go, "Have you thought of any excuse yet to visit the shop this evening?"

I did not know whether to be more embarrassed or vexed at what he said. It was true that during these evening hours, when eminent men were most likely to visit the bookshop, I found many errands that took me there. I had not realized that my true purpose was so easily guessed.

I spoke coldly to Will. "I have no wish to intrude upon matters that do not concern me."

"I commend your modesty. Curiosity in a woman is vulgar. Can you guess who will drink this wine?"

"How could it matter to me?"

"Mr. Otway."

"Thomas Otway, the playwright?"

I could not have pretended indifference if I had tried. I had never met Mr. Otway, who was not one of our authors, but I knew him by reputation. He was said to be a slave to his passions, for he had a hopeless love for Mrs. Barry, the actress, and wrote roles for her in plays so bawdy that I had not yet been allowed to see one; and besides that, he had fought a duel with Mr. Churchill, in which both men had been wounded, and furthermore, he drank far too much wine and was always in great debt.

"Indeed. Of course, it is not a matter that concerns you. I am sure you have no need to visit the shop tonight." And he went smiling from the room.

Toby could not finish his supper fast enough for me. When he was done, he declared that he was still hungry, but I promised him a treat at his breakfast and hastened him to his bed; I was in such a rush I did not even ask to hear his prayers, and, thank God, he did not remember them either.

Then I nearly ran downstairs to the shop—only to see the coat of a man disappearing through our doorway into the evening's last light.

My father was filling his pipe. "You are a moment too late," he said to me. "Thomas Otway, the playwright, was with us just now. What is it, Meg, what do you need?"

Will was lighting the candles, and said nothing, but

though he did not look at me I could see his mocking smile all the same.

There was nothing else to do. I drew in breath, and told my father how I planned to help raise Edward's ransom.

"There are surely more than a hundred parishes in London," my father said. "You cannot visit all."

"It does not matter if I visit all, so long as the ransom is raised."

"I will go to some of the churches," Will said. "I am used to walking about London."

I turned to look at him, astonished, but my father said only, "Good, then. I am pleased to see in both of you this proof of your benevolence."

I wondered, as I returned to the house, what was in Will's mind, and why he had offered to help. He knew Edward only a little; he had not played parlor games with him, as I had, nor watched him triumph over mathematical puzzles when he was but a boy. Certainly he had no guilt to drive him, as I did. Again and again I told myself it was but chance that Edward's vessel had fallen to piracy. But what does it mean to say that something is owed to chance, when we do not know what governs chance itself?

I cannot tell how many curates there are in London. I did not see them all, but I saw many, and each one unlike the next. I saw them old and young, pock-marked and velvet-skinned, bewigged and bald. Each had his own thoughts about captivity in North Africa. One said it was better to labor in Muhammadan Algiers than in Papist Spain. One thought we should form an alliance with the Dutch and wage war upon the Turks. Another was concerned about the temptations a young man might face if exposed to the harems there. But all wanted to know my connection with Edward Gosse.

"Is he your brother, Madame Moore?" Reverend Bradshaw of St. Giles asked me anxiously.

"Not my *brother*," I said, dropping my eyes.

At St. Mildred I had said I was a friend to the family, and the curate had speedily lost interest. I hoped Reverend Bradshaw would make his own guesses, but, like so many clergymen, he was not shy.

"You are betrothed?"

I nodded, keeping my gaze down, and then dabbed at my eye with my gloved finger, as though there were a tear there.

"I will do my utmost for you," the curate said soberly, and I smiled gratefully.

I had high hopes of Reverend Bradshaw, and on the next Sunday, between services, I hurried to Fleet Street that I might find out what kind of collection he had taken in Edward's cause. But as I came to St. Giles I saw Will coming out of it. I tried to read in his face if our luck had been good, but it showed nothing.

He saw me and stayed his step, so I walked on to meet

him. "Did you come on account of the Charity Brief?" I asked.

"I did."

"And was the collection good?"

"It was."

He began walking again, with a long stride, and I hurried that I might not be left behind. "Is something amiss?" I asked, for he seemed almost angry.

He stopped once more. "Did you tell Reverend Bradshaw that you and Edward Gosse are betrothed?"

For a wild moment I thought that he admired me, and was jealous of Edward. But then I looked at the disdain in his face and knew it could not be. I wondered if he would tell my father what I had done, but I scorned to ask him. Instead I lifted my chin and said, "I did."

"And did you lie to him, or to me?"

"To him."

"You are not betrothed to Edward Gosse?"

"I am not."

We began walking again. "You lied to a clergyman," he said. "I worry about the condition of your soul, Madame Moore."

"You worry about *my* soul! *You* are the one who stays out playing cards and drinking ale every night!"

"I drink wine, not ale. Do you think I am a servant? If you are not betrothed to Mr. Gosse, why do you work so hard to bring him home?"

"Why do you?"

He looked at me with a seriousness he did not often show. "I will tell you, if you first tell me."

"Well, then, it is because I am a friend of Anne's."

"Of course." His seriousness had gone; his mouth mocked.

"And you?"

"Why, that your father might approve of me."

I looked at him doubtfully.

"You did not think it was because I so admire Edward Gosse, did you?"

There was a sting in this that I did not expect. "Is there some reason you should *not* admire him?"

Once more his aspect changed, and he spoke soberly. "Of course not. I know nothing but good of him, and I hope we may soon bring him safely home. But it will not hurt me if your father is pleased by my good works. Remember that he holds my future in his hands."

"You could have no better master."

"Certainly not. And now we have told each other all, and you know how eagerly I seek your father's good opinion, and I know—what a great friend you are to Anne."

I knew what he thought—that I loved Edward, even if we were not betrothed. But as I dared not tell him the truth about my thoughtless jest, I made no answer.

"I hope for the sake of his family that our work is not in vain," Will continued. "But it is strange that there has been no letter from him yet. It is possible that he will be one of the many captives who do not come home again."

"Edward would never turn renegade!"

"I know nothing of that. But when you join hard use to a foreign clime, there are many ways to die."

I missed my footing, and stumbled, and Will seized me by the arm to steady me. We had come to Smithfield Market, where the cattle lowed, and the smell of beasts hung in the air. I felt sickened and weary.

"He is not dead," I said.

"Take my arm, madame," was Will's reply, and I held it as we walked on.

I did not think that Edward Gosse was dead. I did not believe that he had died of cannon fire or snakebite or the lash; I did not believe that he had caught the plague or wasted away. With such a ransom at stake, even the cruelest men were bound to take every care. And there were so many other possible fortunes! I had told Will that Edward would never turn renegade, yet scores of Englishmen had done so. And though in plays such renegades came to a bad end, I could not help remembering the many verses written about the pirate John Ward, who lived out his days in a palace in Tunis after he became a follower of Muhammad.

There were many temptations for a Christian in Muslim lands. I dared for a moment to think about the sweetest of these: the enchanting beauty of Muslim women. I had read a story by Mademoiselle de la Roche-Guilhen that described the intrigues of a Turkish harem, so on this point I was well informed. Edward was an able merchant who could speak several languages; he might be very useful in the society of his captors. Surely they would offer him every enticement. He had been enslaved nearly seven weeks. How long could he stand against such persuasions?

That night I lay long awake, imagining different fates for Edward, and after a while, as so often happened, I was not having thoughts, or even seeing pictures, but was stringing words together like beads upon a necklace. The next day, when I was supposed to be helping Betty shine the candlesticks, I sneaked instead into the empty parlor and began to write.

3

All who knew him agreed that Anthony Walters was well favored. His family were prosperous and respected merchants; he was fair of face and quick of wit; he was a capable youth and a prudent one, able to please wherever he went. Before his twentieth year he had so impressed his father that he was dispatched to the Mediterranean to purchase some Indian silks. The business was speedily completed, and Anthony set sail for England, confident of seeing soon the beloved faces of his family.

But his stars cast their malicious influence over the sea as he sailed, and his vessel was overtaken by Turkish pirates . . .

Then I wrote about the fierce efforts of the Turks to turn Anthony from his Christian faith, and how, when he remained steadfast, they forced him to labor like a beast, and finally, how he was given a glimpse of his master's daughter, the beautiful Almira, in her harem clothes and beribboned tresses, which for the first time made him consider the possibility of casting aside all he had been taught.

> *How could a youth of valor and honor have been so tempted? Did no English visage haunt his slumber, that might have kept him from dreaming instead of Almira? There was one—a London maid, to whom he had offered his heart before he left his native shores. But she had not been kind, and if once or twice her image came to him in a dream, it brought with it a bitter perfume . . .*

In the end I could not save him. I tried, but Anthony Walters seemed to have been fated from the story's start to lose his eternal salvation. I consoled myself that at least while on earth he would have great happiness: spices and silks and female beauty at his command. I hoped it was what he wanted.

I did not write "Temptation in Algiers" in a single morning. I could not get much time to myself on the best of days, and even when I had the minutes, sometimes I only sat tapping my fingers against my chin and thinking furiously. I made two false starts, and three false conclusions, and wrote a description of Anthony's encounter with another Christian slave at the mill that went for two pages, and then took it out again. But I did not grow tired of it, as

I had done with some things I had tried to write in the past. Indeed, I thought of it at all hours; it was like a fever upon me. It was what they say love is like.

While I worked, I did not care that my father had forbidden me to show my work to others; I did not think I would ever care. The exhilaration of writing it was enough. Reverend Little, no doubt, would say I was prideful, but it was not like that. It was like having found a whole guinea in the street, and deciding with excitement how to spend it: ten shillings for gifts and good works, perhaps, and the other eleven for poetry and histories—and a pair of scented gloves.

But once I had finished, and the last ink had dried, suddenly having written it was no longer enough, and I ached to share it with someone. For what is the purpose of preparing a great feast, and making all the seasonings right, and putting it upon the table, that it may lie untasted? And yet, even if my father had not forbidden it, to whom could I have shown such a piece? Surely not to Anne! Not to my father, nor to Susannah. Would Mr. Winter look upon the story with friendly eyes? I remembered his displeasure with the first scene I had set in Algiers, and was not easy at the thought. Who, then? No one, after all. I hid the pages inside a book and the book beneath my bed, and fixed my thoughts once more on the redemption of Edward Gosse.

But "Temptation in Algiers" had altered my fears and fancies. I no longer trembled imagining Edward's agonies; now I clenched my fist with jealousy, imagining his desires. For when Anthony fell in love with the beautiful Almira, and forgot the English maid, I cried, not for the hero's sake, but for the maid's. Another in my place would have believed herself in love, I think, simply from the violence of these feelings. For me, however, it was as though I saw myself in a mirror—clenching my fist, and shedding tears—and knew I was but playing a part, one that I had written for myself. It gave me greater ease to suffer than to imagine Edward suffering.

Then I had a letter from Anne, and the play ended. The curtain fell, and I could not pretend anymore.

Five

━ I ━

Anne's letter was sealed with black wax, but I supposed that was for her father—surely it was for her father. I broke the seal quickly and read the note through. It was brief, only asking me to come to her that afternoon as she served at the Three Bells. I was uneasy as I folded the page again. Were there tidings of Edward? Bad tidings, that she did not want to put onto paper?

Will kept the shop that afternoon while I went to Cheapside. In the past few days the weather had grown warm, and the stench of the night-soil that had fallen from the dung carts grew stronger under the beating sun. But today a breeze came up from the river, and lessened the heat and the reek. Shop signs creaked on their chains, and the manes of the horses lifted. I passed a woman selling cauliflowers from a basket upon her head, and the knife-grinder, who went street to street crying his business. A coach rattled by, and a messenger on horseback trotted past in a great hurry. The city was stirring, and I was myself bestirred.

Anne was behind the bar as I came in, handing a tankard to the potboy, who hurried off with it to one of the inner rooms. When I saw the brightness the sight of me brought to her worried face, my very blood jumped with the relief of it, for she could not look happy if he was dead.

"I am so glad to see you!" she exclaimed.

"And I am glad to be here."

"Then do not stand at the bar, but sit with me and have some wine."

I put a hand into the placket that slit my skirt, searching for my pocket, which was hid beneath.

"After all the work you have done in Edward's cause, do you think I would let you pay for your own claret?" Anne demanded. "Sit down."

So we sat together at a table near the door, where Anne could greet her customers as they entered, while the potboy drew the wine.

"How is Mr. Rushworth?" I asked.

She shrugged. "The same. My gowns are too plain, my voice is too loud, my meals are too rich. But while I work here, he dines from home most days, anyway."

"And—and the nights? Are the nights the same as well?"

For a moment she did not take my meaning.

"Does he stay late at the alehouse still?" I asked.

"He does not stay so late," she allowed with a smile.

"Ah!"

"But I did not write to you that I might tell you about my nights! We have had a letter."

"From your brother himself?"

"From himself."

"And—is he well?"

"No, Meg. He is not well." She brought out her own pocket. I had seen it before, and knew she had embroidered it herself: a dark horse with golden bells in its mane. I looked at it and thought, why did I not ask Edward to bring me some such pretty thing? A pocket, or scented gloves, or a lace neckerchief? And I answered myself: *Because then he would believe me willing.*

Anne passed to me the thin sheet of paper she had taken from her pocket. "I cannot bear to read it again myself," she said.

I lifted the page so that the light from the window would fall upon it. I had never seen his hand before. His script was graceful, but writ very large, as though to fill the page as quickly as he could.

Loving and kind Mother, my humble duty unto you. I pray always for your health and that of all my family. My own health is poor but not yet broken. I do not know how much longer it can last, however. My captors are displeased that my ransom has not come before now. I know that the sum is very great, and I am certain you are doing all you can to raise it. But I cannot help urging upon you such haste as is possible. You do

*not know the conditions under which I suffer. I will
not be more explicit. If you cannot send the ransom, at
least do not deny me your prayers, and such words of
encouragement and comfort as my family can send—
or anyone who may be thinking of me. What I chiefly
need (beyond the ransom) is fortitude to bear this dire
captivity. May God be gracious in granting it.*

Your loving son, Edward Gosse

I did not cry. I folded the letter and held it out to Anne
without a word.

"You must keep it. You must show it to the curates you
speak with."

It was then I dropped the letter on the table and put
my face in my hands.

"I know. It is hard to bear," Anne said. "Perhaps as hard
for you as for us."

I lifted my head and looked at her. She was watching
me closely. "You have come to love him since he has been
gone, have you not?" she asked. "That is why you work so
hard on his behalf."

I was unable to conceal my dismay. "Is it not enough
that he is dear to you, and that you are dear to me?" I
asked.

She looked at me as though I had stolen her pocket
from her. "What is *wrong* with him? He is young and vig-
orous, he is courteous, he is able, he is prosperous! What do
you look for in a husband, that he has not? I only wish *I*
could have married as fine a man as my brother!"

I saw that she was near to tears, and wished that I could tell her what she longed to hear. In truth, I almost wondered that I did *not* love Edward. How could a heart be so hard as to fail to love an Englishman enslaved by Turks on the Barbary Coast? A heart as cold as mine was nearly a matter for poetry.

"There is nothing wrong with him," I said gently. "I have never known a boy as pleasing and amiable as Edward. But I fear that growing up at the sign of the Star has spoiled me for marriage. I could not endure being parted from that world—from great minds and new ideas and everything put down on pages. I could not bear to serve wine at the Three Bells and see nothing written down all day except the price of a cup of claret."

I saw by her face that I had gone too far, and hurt her.

"I know you do not like to come here," she said.

"Nonsense. I am grateful for the hospitality you offer, and so are many others. I do not say that what you do is not of value. Only that my heart longs for another world."

Even as I spoke I felt the weakness of what I said. How many among us are granted the lives we long for? And surely we should be governed by our duties, and not by our desires. I knew how selfish my words must sound to Anne, for that was how they sounded in my own ears.

But she did not reproach me. Instead she looked into her cup, and said, almost as though she excused herself, "It is hard for us, that we cannot free him from his suffering. Since we do not send the ransom, I wanted to send hope, instead."

Was there ever such inducement to let a lie be told on one's behalf? I could not help but think of poor Anthony in my story, without the love of an English maid to protect him. "Say what you will," I exclaimed, almost angrily. I stood and put the letter in my pocket. "Say what you must. Do you think I am heartless?"

But I saw in her disconsolate face that she would not offer to her brother hope that was only counterfeit.

<center>~~~ 2 ~~~</center>

As my story had haunted me all the previous week, now I was haunted by phrases from Edward's letter, and especially by all that he had not said. *I will not be more explicit.* I no longer tried to imagine his circumstances: neither his sufferings nor his temptations. There was no need; he had already told me all I could bear to know.

And so it was that my fear turned to rage, which I carried around with me like a large and heavy parcel that could not be set down. It kept me from merriment when jests were told. It kept me from curiosity when I heard a man describe to my father how blood from one dog had been put into the veins of another. Because of it I could not feel humility when I heard sermons preached at church, nor patience when the nightmare woke Toby three times in one night.

"Stop it, stop it!" I said to him as he wept. "It is but a dream; it cannot hurt you. You are too warm, that is all." I felt his gown, and found it moist. Then I pulled up his nightcap and touched his forehead, anxiously, to be sure he had no fever, but thank God, he had none.

"We must change your nightshirt," I said. I drew the bed curtains so as to have a little light from the lantern that burned on the chair nearby.

"It is *not* a dream," he cried. "It is *not*. Do not make me go with Bridget today, Meg, I beg you, I beg you, for today only, let me stay with you in the shop!"

I was surprised, for he used not to like the shop. But in truth, I did not want him with me, for I meant to go to St. Giles again, and show Edward's letter to Reverend Bradshaw. "No, Toby," I said as I began to pull his nightshirt from him—but it stuck to his skin, and now in the faint light I could see a dark stain upon the cloth that clung to his buttock.

Of course there were blows. Every child must suffer blows, until obedience is learnt. But a child need not be beaten until the blood runs.

I wanted to rouse the house. I wanted to pummel Bridget with the broom until she had welts all over her body; I wanted to hear her scream with pain; I wanted to kick her out the door this minute, and hurl her few things after her. I felt I could not bear my own anger, which leaped in my veins until I gave a great shudder and a little cry, and Toby looked up at me fearfully. Then I gathered him into my arms, and petted him, and soothed him, and showered him with apologies and promises, and finally shed a few tears into his silky hair.

We went downstairs to the kitchen, where Betty slept upon a pallet. I woke her and told her what I had found. Her angry hisses soothed me, while together we used water to dampen the cloth of Toby's nightshirt until it could be pulled from him without great pain. Betty lit a candle from the kitchen fire and held it for me while I examined the child's body. Besides his scored flesh, there were many bruises upon his skin. In the stillroom, where Susannah prepared household remedies, I found an ointment for his wounds, and another for his bruises. At last I dressed him in a clean nightshirt and took him back to bed.

"May I stay with you in the shop tomorrow?" he whispered through the dark.

"You need never stay with Bridget again," I promised him.

I should not have made such a promise, for the management of servants was not in my hands. But I was not afraid that I would fail him. I knew that *this*, at least, was an act within my power.

The next morning I did not take Toby to Bridget but to my father. He looked, and he listened, but I could not make him feel the wrath that I felt. "I had worse than that when I was a boy," he said. "Toby must not grow up a weakling."

"It is she who makes him a weakling! He does not know safety even in his own house—how can he dare to face the world?"

"By learning to face his nurse."

"What does it mean to face someone who can do you

great harm in spite of all that you can do to prevent it? Did you face your father, when he beat you for reading when you ought to have been working?" I had heard him tell this story of his childhood many times.

"I learned to read in secret, at least."

"And so from beatings we learn to deceive. In truth, Father, I think deception is an easy enough lesson that it might be learned from gentler teachers."

"You are impertinent, Meg," my father replied, but I heard amusement in his voice.

"A nurse who cannot govern her anger is a danger," I continued. "What if one day she goes too far, and he is lamed, or even killed? Such things happen. It would be but small comfort to dismiss her then."

"I do not think she is so bad as that," my father said, "But it is hardly worth keeping her if she upsets the entire household. I will tell Susannah she may do as she likes."

"Thank you, Father."

"But, Daughter—you know that turning Bridget out will not spare Edward Gosse a single lash."

"Yes, sir," was all that I said, and went quickly away, for I disliked that he knew I hated Bridget all the more because I had no power over the tyrants in Barbary.

When Susannah had seen Toby's wounds it was she who pummeled Bridget. But she landed only a blow or two before my father stopped her, for fear she should injure the babe she carried. Then Bridget was gone, and for a few days all was chaos, so I could not work in the shop, nor go abroad seeking donations for Edward's ransom. Instead I

spent every minute with Toby and with Eleanor, who was a
great bother, for she was cutting a tooth. She had a chain
that was hung with a piece of polished coral for her to bite
upon, but it did not keep her from fretting, and I was glad
that we found a new nurse quickly. Joanna was slow-witted,
but very kind, and my father resigned himself to having a
son who was, if not more manly, at least a great deal happier than he had been.

~~ 3 ~~

As my father had guessed, sending Bridget away did not
lessen my hatred of the Turks. Instead, it grew, until I
gave it voice on an afternoon in September, when Mr.
Winter came into the shop. Will had gone to see the vicar
of St. Mary-le-Bow—so he said, and he had Edward's letter
in his pocket. I was certain he would spend most of his
time idling with other apprentices whose masters placed
overmuch trust in them, but I was too weary to question
him closely. What did it matter what he did with his time?
When first we began to visit London parishes, the shillings
poured in, and when we shared Edward's letter there was
another spate of giving, though not as great as we hoped.
For the sake of his ransom, it would have been better if he
had chosen to be explicit, after all. We were yet twelve
pounds from our goal—so little that generous gifts from a
handful of wealthy men would bring Edward home. Yet it
seemed we could not squeeze another farthing from anyone

in London Town. Everyone had heard the story, everyone had given what he could; some had given twice, or thrice. Now they wanted only to be left in peace.

So ran my thoughts that afternoon in September when Mr. Winter entered the shop. I do not know if it was the hatred or the despair that showed in my face, but something did, for when he saw me he did not call me "madame," as he had done since I returned from my studies in Herefordshire, but burst out, "Why, Meg, what ails you?"

I looked at him for a moment as though I did not know him. I held a dustcloth in one hand and a stack of unbound pages that I had lifted from the table in another, but I hardly remembered that I had been dusting, my thoughts had been so far from what I did. I set the pages down upon the table and said, "The same thing that ails me every day. The suffering of Edward Gosse."

He fished in his pocket for a crown and set it on the counter as I took my place there, but that did not get us much nearer.

"I *hate* these accursed Turks," I said as I brought out the ledger. "I abominate them! I wish that every Algerine ever born may die in torment and spend eternity in the flames of hell!"

"You must calm yourself," Mr. Winter said gravely. "That is no way for a Christian to speak. You must pray for their salvation."

"Why do they hate us so? It is because they know we are saved, and they are damned!"

"In fact, they believe the opposite."

"But they are wrong!" I spoke as though I had poison on my tongue, that could wreak harm on Edward's captors so far away. "Muhammad was nothing but a cobbler, who cobbled together some things he was told by Jews and Papists and made it into a religion."

"A Muslim might say that Our Lord was only a carpenter, who patched together a house out of stories told by Jews."

"You defend them. You defend these vile pirates, these thieves, these *devils* who keep slaves to serve them, as though men were beasts."

"I do not defend them," he protested. He began to walk up and down before the fire, as though it helped him to think. "Slavery is an abomination. But they are not the only people in the Mediterranean who practice piracy. The Spanish and the Portuguese have enslaved thousands of Moors, branding them, chaining them to galleys. What country's galleys have not been rowed by slaves? The Maltese, the Italians, the French—all have been rowed by North African slaves."

"There are no English galleys," I argued.

"We are not a Mediterranean power." He stood now before the fire, with his hands clasped behind him. "But in our King's father's reign English jails were crowded with Moors and Turks, and many were sold to the Spanish as slaves. Others were executed as pirates."

"They *were* pirates."

Mr. Winter shrugged. "Some may have been. But there

are lords who have bought Turkish boys, and keep them in livery to wait upon their ladies, not a mile from where we sit." He pointed as he spoke, as though I could see through our window to the fine houses where these Turkish boys lived. "And what of the African slave trade? Think of the Negroes who are shipped to the West Indies to work on the plantations there. That slavery is on our heads."

"That is different! They are only brutes!"

"Did you chance to read a work published last year by Morgan Godwyn, of Oxford? He calls it *The Negro's and Indian's Advocate*."

I shook my head.

"A pity. In it he asks, if a Briton is enslaved by an Algerine, does he at that moment become a brute? If not, why must it be that an African becomes a brute the moment he is enslaved?"

"They are not Christians," I said stubbornly.

"Even if they should embrace our faith, it does not change their condition of servitude," Mr. Winter said. "But if an Englishman embraces Islam, then he is set free. I have heard that the rights of slaves are enumerated in the Qur'an, the holy book of Muhammad. I have not read it myself, I admit. But there is an English version, done by Alexander Ross from a French translation of the Arabic. It is sold by Randal Taylor, I believe, near the Stationers' Hall. Perhaps it would ease you to look into it."

I did not answer.

"If I bring you a copy, will you read it?"

I could not believe that he asked it of me. "I would not have their filthy book in my shop!"

"A pity. You used to read so widely. What do you read now, madame?"

He had been my friend for many years. He had been the one who encouraged me, while my father only scolded me. But now there was no difference between the one and the other; both set themselves up to criticize what I read and what I wrote.

"I have not had much leisure for reading of late," I said, which was very true. "I have been working to ransom Edward Gosse."

He was briefly silent, then burst out, "Forgive me, Meg! I forgot for a moment how much you are suffering on that poor boy's account." He reached in his pocket again, and this time drew out a guinea. "I find I do not need a new periwig, after all," he said, and held the coin out to me. I opened my palm to receive it, and he clasped my hand between his own. "Say that you forgive me, madame, for I am not the Turk, you know, but an old friend who has argued with you many times before now."

I could not speak, but only nodded.

"I will pray that God will relieve you of this burden," he said, and went away without buying anything.

But I knew that nothing would relieve me until Edward Gosse was home again, and in that moment I resolved that I would do whatever daring thing I must to procure the rest of his ransom.

D aughter, where are you bound? Where do you go dressed like that?" my father asked.

If he had been in the shop, I would have got out unmarked, except by Deb, who helped me dress. Alas, he had stepped into the house for a moment to speak to Susannah, and was just returning, so we met at the door as I reached to take my cloak from its peg.

I wore my newest and finest gown, the one I had bought for Anne's wedding, and had never put on since. It was of indigo silk, with an underskirt of pale blue and an abundance of lace at the cuffs and bosom, and many sweet velvet bows upon the skirt. Not only that, but I had stolen into Susannah's cabinet and used her crayons to paint my face—blue for the eyelids, and red for the lips. I did not paint my cheeks, as they were always apt to show too much of the rose, rather than too little. I did, however, affix to one cheek two patches of Susannah's—a small red leather heart and a black crescent moon.

No wonder that he asked me where I was bound. He knew I was not going out to buy turnips.

I could not think of a single story except the truth. "I go to see the King, sir," I said.

"What can you mean?"

"I will wait for him in St. James's Park, where he walks so often. If I have the good fortune to meet with him, I will petition him for the rest of Edward's ransom."

"You are wasting your time."

"I do not care. I must try something."

He opened the door to the shop and called to Will. I almost bit my lip in dismay—I did not want Will to mock me in my finery—but I remembered in time that if I did so, the paint would be spread all about my mouth.

Will came to us, and my father said to him, "Meg wishes to wait in St. James's Park on the chance of seeing the King. You will go with her."

"Yes, sir."

"I may go?" I asked with astonishment.

"If you have courage enough to face the King, I will not prevent you." He turned and went into the shop.

Will held the door to the street open for me. I kept my eyes turned from him. For once he did not tease and chatter as we walked, and I was glad for whatever thought kept his tongue quiet.

It was near to Michaelmas, which comes in late September, and begins the new term. The sky was the gray of goose feathers, and the wind was keen, but it had not rained for many days and the streets were dry, for which I thanked God, for otherwise my dress would have been ruined. In Holborn, Will hailed a hackney coach, and when we were side by side within I finally dared to glance at him. He was looking at me, and what I saw in his eyes was not mockery.

I looked hastily away—into my lap, at my hands in their embroidered gloves. How long had he been looking at me thus? Had he looked at me in that way at Anne's wedding, when I had worn this gown? I could not recall; I hardly remembered seeing him there. But I remembered all the times he had watched me so closely, and suddenly I saw them differently. I felt as though I stood looking at a frozen river as the thaw came; the landscape changed as I watched, and all that I had believed hard and true now moved and shifted before me.

The wheels of the hackney made a terrific din against the cobbles, but between us was a silence that neither of us dared to break. The jostling of the coach threw us toward one another, but our shoulders did not touch. At last I could not bear it, and began to speak, awkwardly, talking of the ransom, and how best to approach the King.

"You will have no trouble attracting his notice," Will said. "He is—he likes . . ."

He did not finish, but I saw what he meant to say, that the King was in love with all the female sex. I knew that I was no great beauty who is talked of throughout the Town because she is so fair. A girl knows such things well before she turns sixteen. But now Will's tongue, that usually ran so freely, stumbled simply because I was near, and for the first time in my life I dared to tell myself that I was pretty.

We came to St. James's Park, and Will handed me down from the coach. I let my gaze linger on his for a moment—only a moment—but he saw what he wanted to see, and was himself again.

"This is where the King plays pall-mall," he said, pointing to the tree-lined avenue before us. "It is covered with powdered cockleshells, that the boxwood ball may roll smoothly when it is struck with a mallet. South of us you see the canal." He pointed to a flat, gray sheet of water in the distance. "The King has brought waterfowl from all over the world to live on the island there. Beyond is Bird-cage Walk, where they keep parrots and cassowaries in gilded cages."

"Does the King walk there?"

"Oh, yes. He takes his dogs around the water, and sometimes he swims there. In winter it freezes, and the Duke of York puts on skates and slides upon the ice."

"But where am I most apt to encounter the King to-day?"

"His common walk is there, to the west." He pointed, and we began to go in that direction.

"I do not think the King will give the whole twelve pounds, if he gives any," Will said. "You will not disgrace me by throwing an orange at him if he refuses you? A man was locked up for that once."

"You are absurd," I said to him, but I could not keep the laughter from my voice. "If he does not help me, I will go elsewhere, that is all. I will go to the most eminent men that have come to the sign of the Star, both the authors and the patrons. I will go to John Dryden, and to Mr. Barker, the astrologist, and to Isaac Newton, and Mr. Otway—"

"Your father will thrash you if you go to Mr. Otway."

"I do not care."

We came to uneven ground, and Will offered me his arm, which I took with one hand, while I used the other to lift my skirt.

"Your father spends much time cultivating learned men. When I have my own shop—"

"You are always talking about having your own shop," I said. "But I do not think your family have the means to set you up in business when your apprenticeship is done."

"They can do something for me, but not all. My wife's dowry must do the rest."

I did not speak for a moment, but looked at the ground as we picked our way over it. As I had foretold, art would have been wasted on my cheeks, which were now painted by nature. His tone was so careless I did not know what to think. At last I said, "I hope for your sake you will find a very rich widow."

"She need not be so very rich. A dowry the size of yours would be sufficient."

I stopped, and turned my gaze upon him. His glance was bright and daring.

"Is it my father's wish?" I asked him, for his words suggested to me that they had spoken together of this.

"That you must ask your father," he replied.

But I did not need to ask. I thought of all the ways my father had favored Will, how he had taken him up like a son and taught him freely the tricks of the trade, and I knew it was not for Will's sake that he did it, but for my own, that I might have the life I longed for. Just then the sun came from behind the clouds, and glinted so brightly upon the canal that my eyes were pricked with tears. A white bird left the water with a beating of wings, then returned with a splash. I could not speak. I looked westward

again, and saw the King's back as he walked briskly away
from us, with a handful of advisers straggling after him. He
had come, and now he had gone. I turned to Will, but he
had not seen the King. He looked only at me.

"We have missed the King," I said. "Now I must go to
Mr. Dryden."

"I will go with you. I will not stop tramping around
this town until you have brought that boy home." He
paused. "There are more than three years left to my term,
you know. Much may happen in that time."

"That does not trouble me."

He looked at me as though trying to read my thoughts.
"When Mr. Gosse has returned to London, then we shall
see."

See what? I thought to myself. Edward was a wine merchant. Will would be a bookseller. There was nothing to
see.

It was during the third week of October that we at last
gained the sum needed to ransom Edward Gosse. I had
kept my resolve, and visited the great men I had met at my
father's shop, beginning with those I knew best, and not
bothering with Mr. Otway. I hoped to make an end to this
work quickly, for I knew if any of them told my father
what I did, he would put a stop to it at once. But it rained
heavily in early October; the streets grew wet and foul, and

it was not easy to traverse them. I hinted to Will that he might go in my stead, for he had boots to bear him through the mire. He said he would, but day after day he put it off, and I saw that he was afraid to face my father's wrath, for which I did not blame him. I was afraid myself. But I could not be easy until I had undone the harm that followed on my thoughtless jest, so at last I put on my oldest gown, wrapped myself in a hooded mantle, and set my slippered feet within the iron loops of the pattens that would carry me through the streets. They were four inches high, with soles of heavy wood. When I wore them it seemed I walked on stilts, and every step upon the wet cobbles felt perilous.

Therefore I did not go quickly—still, I went. In the end I saw two of my father's prized authors and five of his best customers, and got what I needed. As soon as I had enough I went to my father and told him what I had done. His anger was nothing light. In its first flare I thought that he would beat me, as he had not done for many years, for without his consent I had used the good name of his business, which was as dear to him as any living thing. At last he calmed himself, however, and commanded me to stay within doors (when not attending church) for fully a month. That meant I could not go to the playhouse, nor to dine with a friend, nor even to buy ink of a crier in the street. And of course I missed the public celebrations—the bonfires and processions of Gunpowder Plot Day, near the start of November, and those of the Queen's birthday in the middle of that month.

I did not fault him, though. If the shop had been my own, and anyone had taken the same liberty with my patrons, I would have given as bad, or worse. And in any case I was greatly needed at home just now, for Susannah was coming near to her time, and must be often waited on in her chamber.

Because I could not leave the house, I sent Will to Mrs. Gosse with the ransom. A few days later I received from Anne this letter:

Dearest friend,
My heart is very full as I write, for I have had three pieces of news in a short time. One came from Edward, who has been sold to another master in Algiers. I do not know whether these tidings are bad or good. But because of the news I have had from you, I was able to send him word, this day, that the ransom is coming at last. It will go first to a Christian merchant in Leghorn, thence to a Jew there, and finally to a Spanish Jew who lives in Algiers, and who has ransomed many Englishmen before now. I cannot thank you enough, good friend, for all that you have done on Edward's behalf.

And now, Meg, I must tell you one last piece of delicious news. I have suspected it for some time, but now it has been nine weeks since my months have come, and so I am certain that I am with child. Mr. Rushworth delights that I am breeding, though I cannot say he carps less on account of it. But I do not care

*one whit! I care only for these twin gifts from God: my
brother and my child, coming to me soon.*

I was glad to hear Anne's news, very glad indeed, but
such a blessing also brings uneasiness. Childbirth is the
greatest danger a woman knows in all her years upon this
earth. It had taken my own mother's life when I was but
eight, and it could as easily take Anne's—or, before that,
Susannah's.

I was very nervous in those weeks, as the year waned
and the afternoons darkened. I felt shy when I found myself alone with Will, and knew not what to say, though I
stole glances at him as though I had never looked at him
before, and satisfied myself that he was handsome enough
to please. I was often restless and agitated; I could not settle on a book to read, nor a story to write. Whatever I did I
wished it quickly done, as though doing something else
would please me better—but nothing did please me. At
dinner one day I picked up a platter of oysters too quickly,
only to see a dozen of them slide onto the table. Betty, who
waited on us, exclaimed sharply, and Deb clapped her hand
over her mouth to stifle a laugh. Will would have laughed,
too, I think, but did not dare. As for my father, he only
motioned at me to pick them up again, which I did anyway, with haste and blushes.

Susannah was not there to see, of course. She did not
come to dinner now, but stayed to her bed, and I spent
more time running up and down the stairs to wait upon

her than I did in the shop. I did not mind, for that way I could be alone with my daydream, and think about what books Will and I might one day publish, and choose what authors we might invite to dine. In fact, I so often went to Susannah's chamber to ask if she was in need that at last she bade me sit beside her bed, and regarded me with a look of perplexity.

"What ails you, Meg? You are nervous as a cat."

"Why, I think only of your comfort."

"You were not like this when I bore Eleanor."

"It is the time of year, perhaps."

"That is no excuse. It is not so many weeks to Christ-mastide. Think how merry we shall all be then."

"And we will have a new child, to celebrate with us."

"God willing," she said with grave face. "You are very dear to me, Meg, do you know?" I did not answer her, but I was much moved, and took her hand in mine. Then she continued, "But I think you seek to deceive me." I stared at her with such honest astonishment that she amended her words. "Or you deceive yourself. I know this mood is not all on my account. It was when your father courted me that I was nervous in the way that you are now. Tell me—I promise I will not say a word to your father. Is it Mr. Gosse you think of, or Mr. Barlow?"

I felt my face redden, and was glad of the candlelight, which revealed so little. I shook my head at her. I did not want to tell her what had passed between Will Barlow and myself in St. James's Park. It was not time; that bread was still dough, and who could say if it would ever rise? Besides, with a secret of this kind, the delicious flavor of it could all too easily be spoilt by advice and regulation.

"A shaken head may mean many things," Susannah said to me when I did not speak. "Keep your counsel, then. You are a good girl, and I am not afraid that you will run away with your lover. There, if you can settle the pillow for me, I will be more comfortable."

And I crept away, feeling somehow both discovered and concealed, and, despite all, much comforted.

By chance, it was late next day that Susannah began her labor, and soon she was surrounded by gossips: her mother and sister and two cousins, and Mrs. Gosse, and of course the midwife came. Only married women were allowed within the birth chamber, and I was not sorry to be excluded. I was afraid, if truth be told—afraid for Susannah and afraid to see what I must endure myself, one day, if indeed I should marry. Eleanor's birth had been swift and easy, so I hoped for the same this time, but the hours wore on and Susannah's groaning was deeper and more anguished than I had heard before, and my fear grew. Then prayer welled up from the deepest place within me, the place lit by God, that is beyond the sins and scars we bear because of Adam. I sat in my chamber with Toby on my lap and petted his hair, and wondered where we find courage. But then I thought: Perhaps we do not find it at all. Perhaps we *are* not brave, and if we had the choice, we would not bear our travails. It is only in looking back, when we have endured what we could not avoid, that everyone says we have been brave.

Susannah screamed with pain, and Toby put his hands upon his ears while the tears ran down his cheeks. "I die! I die!" she cried out.

But she did not, thank God. Instead, the child came at last from her womb, and was washed in warm wine and rolled in soft cloths, and was laid in his cradle. I was let into the chamber then, and kissed Susannah's brow, which still shone with the sweat of her labor. And seeing her sweat, and the tears that were yet upon her cheeks, I thought differently, and it seemed to me she had shown great courage, in spite of having had no choice in the matter.

Anne had told me that she hoped Edward would be redeemed by Christmas, but it was not so. It slowed things that the ransom must pass through so many hands, and contrary winds were also at work. We learned later that it was as the bells in London churches rang in the year of 1682 that Edward's ransom at last reached his master. And then he was advised by the English consul to await a convoy, as it had happened before that a ransomed captive left one North African port, only to be seized by another power— by Morocco, perhaps, or Tripoli. Of course, we did not know all this at the time. We knew only that the days passed. My new brother was christened Harold, and a few weeks afterward was freed from his swaddling bands and had his little arms put into sleeves for the first time.

Christmas Day came with its mince pies, and Twelfth Night with its cake. My slice had the pea within it, which meant I was Queen of the revels, and I waited in excitement and alarm to see which boy would find the bean and be my King. I did not want it to be Will, for fear that anyone seeing us together would know our secret. But in spite of that I was disappointed when it was not, and I saw from his face that he felt the same.

After Twelfth Night the Town grew quiet, as though exhausted by merriment. Anne began to fret because there was no word of Edward, and Mrs. Gosse was distracted with anxiety. Even my father wondered aloud what had gone wrong.

But I did not fret. I was like a butterfly who has been held between cupped hands and then let go; it flies swiftly hither and thither, delighting in its freedom. I was foolish and giddy, made jests upon all subjects, teased my father to buy me new ribbons, and fixed extra bows to my gowns upon the least occasion. If someone had asked me how I could be so blithe in the midst of such uncertainty I would have said: I am done worrying always about Edward Gosse! In truth, though I had imagined so many terrible fates for him in the past, I could not now imagine that he would fail to come safely to England's shores.

Indeed, I did not like to think overmuch of his coming. I did not want to see him; I did not even like him. It was as though I resented him for his suffering. He was no longer Anne's brother, whom I had known for so long; he was not the youth who had courted me. He was only someone I had wronged—and to whom I had made restitution.

It was now over three months since Will and I had waited for the King in St. James's Park, and not one word on the subject of marriage had passed between us. But one day toward the end of January, as we were together in the shop, Will said from behind the counter, "When I have my own business, I will sell more books of jests."

I looked up from my task—I was on my knees, delving into a low cupboard to see which books had sat there so long unsold. "Jests will always be popular," I agreed.

"And not so many stories of exotic times and places," he added slyly.

"You must ask your wife what she thinks of that plan!" The words were out of my mouth before I thought, and then my cheeks reddened, and I wished I had not spoken.

But Will looked pleased. "That matters not. I will be the head of the business, not she."

I saw that he meant to provoke me, as he had done so many times, but how differently it struck me now! I shut the cupboard door and got to my feet. "So you intend to live at war with your wife, instead of at peace?" I asked as I wiped my hands upon a handkerchief.

"Perhaps I will not choose to live at war, but I do not know that I am averse to a little battle," he said, and I could not keep from laughing.

Mr. Winter entered at that moment. "What a pleasure

it is to hear your laughter," he said when he had made his bow. "Things go better with you, now that Edward Gosse is bound for London."

His mistake embarrassed me, and I knew not what answer to make. "I am foolish today," I said at last. "I laugh at nothing."

"Laughter needs no excuse," Mr. Winter said with a smile. "I have heard that your father will reprint the poems of 'Ephelia' soon, is it true? I want to send them to a friend, and do not like to lose my own copy."

It was Will who answered. "That is his plan, but it is not done yet. Can I persuade you to buy the work of another poet instead? Perhaps one of our own sex, for the worst words writ by a man will outshine the best by a woman, you know."

"Shame upon you, sir, for saying such things before Madame Moore!" Mr. Winter scolded. "I see you have not read her verses."

Will looked at me with surprise. "Her verses?" he repeated.

"I have written dozens," I confessed. "It passes the time."

"I am sure they are charming," Will said courteously, but he did not smile.

Mr. Winter looked from my face to Will's. He said nothing, but even so I was abashed, for he had defended me to Will, but I had not defended myself. I remembered my father saying I would make myself a laughingstock, and was cast down, for now I saw that Will had laughed with him at female authors, and my father had spoken as he did that I might not ruin my chance at a good match. I felt wretched, and wished for anything, even fire or flood, that might distract the minds of these two men.

It was then that my father entered the shop. "Why do you look so sour, Daughter?" he asked me when he had greeted Mr. Winter. "Never mind, you will rejoice when you hear my news. The first ship of the convoy that brings Edward Gosse back to London has been sighted from Gravesend. You and Mr. Barlow have both worked hard for this day."

Will turned quickly toward me, as though he thought there was something to be learned from my face, but there was not.

"Well, *that* story is over," was all I said, which was true enough.

"Only think what he has lived through since he left these shores," said Mr. Winter. "He has a tale to tell."

And that was true as well.

1682

Six

⚊ I ⚊

It was a dark winter day, and I had spent most of the afternoon in the shop with my father, while Will sold books from a stall in St. Paul's Churchyard. At first we had many customers, for we had lately published a tragedy about the Earl of Essex that had been acted at the Theatre Royal, and it was selling well, chiefly because the prologue and epilogue had been written by Mr. Dryden. But as the day grew colder and darker, fewer came into the shop. My father lit the candles early, so that we might have enough light to read when there were no customers by, but I hardly knew what volume to take in my hand. At last I picked up a play by Mr. Dryden. I had read it many times before, but when I am ill at ease, I find that nothing gives as much comfort as a story with no surprises in it. And I had no ease that day, for though Mrs. Gosse had written to me when Edward had come safely to Broad Street, and said that I should dine with them when he had recovered from his journey, I felt I could not be perfectly comfortable until we met.

It was nearly nightfall when Will returned. I looked up at once when the door opened, wondering if he remembered tomorrow's date, and if he did, whether he would mention it.

He came into the room and set upon the counter a short stack of unsold books.

"I see business was good today," my father said, and put his own reading down upon the counter.

"Yes, sir," Will said, and handed over the shillings he had carried home in his purse.

My father counted them out, and looked over the titles to see what had sold and what had not, and nodded at Will in a way that showed he was well pleased. Then he took the till with him and went upstairs, leaving Will and me to bar the door.

"He thinks you are a clever bookseller," I said to Will when my father had gone.

"Indeed I am. I persuaded an old man to buy again a book that I sold to him a week ago."

"For shame, Mr. Barlow, what would my father say?"

"Do you not yet know when I am in jest?"

He was smiling, but I could not tell if indeed he *had* been in jest, or if he now daubed himself with whitewash.

Before I could speak he turned the subject. "I sold much poetry today—it is the season, you know. I even sold some verses writ by one of your sex. It is a wonder what people will buy."

"People of intelligence, yes. *They* will certainly be open to authors of all kinds."

We had made no mention of my writing since the day Will had learned about it from Mr. Winter, but we sparred with one another in this manner to show we were not bothered by our differing views on the subject.

"You must come to the shop tomorrow morning, as early as you can, if you please," Will said to me. "There is a task that needs your attention, but it is too late to begin it tonight. I will be at work early, and will direct you."

In the past his voice had rankled when he spoke thus, but now it made me smile, for I knew he remembered that tomorrow was St. Valentine's Day, and he meant to be the first man I saw, which would make him my valentine. I wondered what sort of gift he would offer me. Of course, it was my birthday, too. My father gave him little to spend, but I knew his family brought him money from Bristol several times each year, that he might buy wigs and waistcoats and sit up late drinking with persons of quality. Gloves? A fan? A locket, that I might carry his hair within it? No, that would go too far. Perhaps only a length of satin ribbon, red, which would look well against the brown of my hair.

I lay abed that night thinking of possibilities, and smiling at the bed curtains until my mouth did ache from my happiness. In the morning I dressed quickly but carefully, and lingered a moment before the glass, to fix a velvet bow to my hair. Then I tumbled my brother into his clothes, and took him to Joanna.

But when I entered the shop there was only my father there.

"You look very pretty today, Child," he said to me as I came into the room. The fire was bright, and the candles were burning, though outside the day had dawned, and the criers had begun calling their wares.

"I am not a child any longer, sir. Today is my seventeenth birthday."

At that he came and kissed me, which he did but seldom.

"Where is Will, Father? Should he not be working at this hour?"

"There is a man selling songbirds in the next street; I heard his cry and sent Will out to buy one, for I must have something to give Susannah besides a set of verses. Do not fret, Meg, he will be back in a moment."

Indeed, the door opened, and I turned toward it with my prettiest smile. But of course it was not Will. Of course it was Edward Gosse instead. I felt a tumult in my stomach, and heat in my face, and I did not understand myself, for I was afraid, but did not know why.

Upon a second glance I was surprised that I had known him, for he did not look like the same man. He had no wig, but wore his hair in a tail tied behind his neck. It had grown lighter in that sun-battered city, and was now the color of straw. He was well dressed, in a velvet suit, but it looked strange upon him, for he was brown as a sailor, and lean, and he had grown a yellow beard that was somewhat overlong. In short, you could see that he was no longer accustomed to fashion. The lost weight he would regain, surely, and his skin would pale in a season, if not sooner. But something had altered in his face that it troubled me to see. I well recollected the timidity, the gentleness, and finally the pain I had seen there last. Now, by the light of the candles in the sconce on the wall, his countenance appeared as unyielding as a door that has been barred for the night.

"Mr. Gosse! We are so glad to see you at last!" my father said, much surprised.

Edward bowed. "I hope I do not disturb you, coming so early."

"Of course not, we are open for business, as you see. I wager you do not even know that it is St. Valentine's Day, and that you have just become Meg's valentine," my father said with good humor. "Now you must give her a present, you know."

Edward turned toward me, and paused irresolutely.

"My father jests with you," I said quickly. "No present is necessary."

"I have brought you a gift, though. I have brought you what you asked for."

I stood wordless, hopeless, waiting for him to speak and my father to hear what I had so mightily repented saying. But to my great joy, the door opened again, and Will entered, holding a caged songbird in one hand. He looked at Edward, and then at me, and I thought his face had never looked so comely—or so careful.

"Ah," my father said. "I must take this sweet creature to my bride." He took the cage from Will and went into the house.

Will bowed quickly. "Mr. Gosse, welcome to our shop—and to our shores. I hope you will not think me rude if I attend to a matter that cannot wait."

And he left me alone with Edward.

"I am surprised to see you," I said. "I thought that we would meet in Broad Street."

"So I thought, as well. But then I resolved to come here, instead. I have something particular to say to you— something to ask you—and I did not want to ask it with all my brothers and sisters listening!"

I was filled with distress to know that I must hurt him more, after what he had been through, but at the same time I felt a blaze of pride to know he had thought of me all those months. "Edward, I am so sorry," I began, but he made a noise that was like laughter, and yet unlike, and I stopped in surprise.

"Do not be afraid," he said. The smile upon his face looked somehow ill humored. "My recent troubles have driven all thoughts of courtship from my mind, I assure you, and even if they had not, I am an orphan now, and may not marry until I come of age, unless the Court of Aldermen should give its consent."

I ought to have blushed for my mistake, because I had

been so immodest, but his last words made me angry, for he spoke as though he did not think the aldermen would approve of me.

"We must understand each other, Meg," Edward continued. "I know—I have been told—how great an instrument you were in obtaining my ransom. That lies between us, before anything more can be said. You have my gratitude."

"It was—it was not—"

"I know what it was not. I have spoken with Anne."

"Why, then, have you come?" I demanded in spite of myself, and was horrified to hear how vexed my voice sounded.

But he did not seem to notice my annoyance. "You told me that you wanted me to bring you a narrative of my captivity."

The moment of reckoning had come at last, and I did not try again to evade it. "I have suffered from that day to this for those words, Edward," I said quietly. "I hardly dare to beg your pardon."

He looked at me for a moment before he replied, and I tried to read his face, but I could not. At last he spoke. "I thought it might be so. You feared that what you said had a part in my fortune?"

"Who can be certain that it did not?"

"I. I am certain."

What a lightening of my spirit those words brought! They took from me a weight I had carried so long I almost did not remember how to walk without it.

" 'Twas only a jest, was it not?" he continued. "I do not believe there was any unkind thought that lay behind your speech, truly wishing ill upon me. Am I wrong?"

"Of course there was not!"

"No harm can come of such foolery, I am sure, beyond a man's hurt feelings. As to that—" He shrugged. "For some blows there are no kind words. In truth—you will find this strange—your jest did some good, and without it I could not have borne what was given to me to bear."

I looked at him with doubt.

"Every day, a dozen times in a day, I said to myself, I must remember this, and when I return to London, I will tell it to Meg. I will tell her all my adventures, and she will write my story."

"You did not think me in earnest!"

"That did not matter. *I* was in earnest."

I saw now what he wanted of me, and began to retreat, as an animal does that fears an encounter, but dares not turn its back. "Then write a history of your captivity, and bring it to my father, he may like to publish it."

He shook his head. "I am no poet. It is for you to turn my journey into art."

"I suppose Anne has told you of my scribbling. But if you had read it you would know it is nothing, you must not regard it. My father will help you with your narrative. He has great experience."

"I have read what you call your scribbling, and I want *you* to be the author of my narrative."

"You have read it!"

"I have been reading it for years. You will not be angry with Anne?"

"For years!" All my silly verses; all the stories stolen from better writers; all the scenes I was so proud of the day they were writ, and could not think of without shame two months later. It was as well for Anne she was not near. But before I could voice my pique, an idea came into my mind that trumped all other feelings. Until this moment I had thought only of my father's wrath if I dared to disobey him—but now I imagined things differently. I imagined having written Edward's narrative for him; I pictured myself showing it proudly to my father; I smelt the ink fresh upon the page, and saw customers coming from all corners of London to buy the gripping tale I had written. I heard my father saying, *Have you another story you are writing, Daughter, that we might sell here at the sign of the Star?*

And I heard Will saying, *It is as fine as if a man had done it.*

"I will not press you," Edward said. "It would ease me to tell you my story, but you do not owe it to me to listen. You have paid your little debt a thousand times over."

So he said, and yet he *did* press me, with the fierceness of his eyes, and the set of his shoulders. I was uneasy, and wondered if he had a plan he was not telling me. But it was a fleeting thought, and could not vie long with the picture of my words upon printed pages.

"Let us not mention it to my father, but surprise him when we are done," I said, and he agreed to this plan.

"I must go now," he said. "They will worry that I have

been abroad so early. And your father is right, you know. I did not realize that today was St. Valentine's Day. So I must attend to that duty, as well."

"It is not necessary." I spoke with resentment, for I thought it unkind in him to say he had not sought to be my valentine, and to call the giving of a gift a duty, as though it were the signing of a contract, or the collection of a debt.

Before the day was out, a messenger came with a cask of Rhenish wine and a couplet that was always passed around at this season. I had read it many times before, and thought to myself that I would rather have had a length of red ribbon from my father's apprentice.

2

You were very quick to leave me alone with Mr. Gosse," I said to Will the next time we were together and without other listeners.

He had been tending the fire, but now straightened and regarded me. "Did you think I would stand about and scowl at him, that he might be discouraged from prosecuting his suit?"

With my finger I followed a long scratch in the oaken counter before me, and with my eyes I followed the finger. "He does not court me. If once he thought of it, he does not think of it now."

"And yet he is barely at home in London before he seeks you out—on St. Valentine's Day."

"He did not know it was the fourteenth."

"Of course he did not." Will turned back to the fire.

"I never thought before that you were slow-witted," I said to his back. "He came to thank me, of course, for my part in his redemption."

He finished his task, and took up the cloth we kept by the hearth to wipe his hands clean of coal dust. "And did you explain to him all I had done to help?" he asked.

I was taken aback, for I had not thought to do this.

"It does not matter," Will said with a mocking smile as he came to take my place behind the counter. "No doubt your father will mention it to him when they next meet."

My father. I liked to think of what he might say when he saw my finished narrative, but I did not like to imagine what would pass if he found me engaged upon the work. I had always known that I was not as dutiful as other daughters, but I had told myself that it was more a matter of ill luck than of willfulness on my part. If I was clumsy with a needle and quick-witted with words, was that my fault? But as I set out to deceive my father in the matter of Edward's narrative, I could no longer hide my wrongness from myself. What can I say on my own behalf, except that I could not withstand the temptation? There are drunkards and lechers, gluttons and gamesters, who might say the same. Is art a vice, then, like any other? And yet no one will speak for the drunkard, while many will speak for the poet.

It was easy to find time for secret meetings with Edward Gosse, for naturally I called frequently upon Anne while she was with child. My family believed that I sat with her for an hour or more on each visit, but the truth was I spared her only a little of that time, and then I met instead with her brother. Anne knew why we met, and had much enthusiasm for our project, though she knew not that I concealed it from those at home.

Edward, more than I, was hard pressed to find time for our meetings, for he had much to do to set the business right. He collected money that was owed him from merchants who had put off Mrs. Gosse many times, and called one of the apprentices who had gone home to the country back to serve the rest of his term. Not all could be as it was, however. Henry Gosse did not return to the apothecary, but continued to help in the business; his brother Peter did not go back to Oxford, but instead studied in Town. As for Edward, his presence was much required in the warehouse, while Mrs. Gosse returned thankfully to the Three Bells.

That was where we met, when Edward could spare an hour or two. Our meetings were often at dinnertime, for even a busy man must eat, and it made as much sense for Edward to dine at the tavern as anywhere else. The little room we used had but one table and two chairs, drawn near to the hearth, and a single window that looked not upon Cheapside but upon a little lane that ran between buildings. I recognized the chairs, which surely replaced the stools ordinarily used; they were from the house in Broad Street. There were two prints upon the walls, one of a ship attacked by a sea serpent, and one that was a map of London that showed what part of it had been burnt in the Great Fire.

I grew to know every detail of that room, each stain upon the wall and each groove carved into the table. Within its confines I learned to see not only the familiar English furnishings, but other sights that hitherto had been unknown to me: the sparkle of the blue Mediterranean, the white rooftops that glinted in the Algerine sun, golden domes and marble pillars and towering minarets. It was always strange to walk into Cheapside after listening to Edward, and to see before me a bewigged man riding by on a horse, when my mind was filled with the picture of a turbaned man upon a camel. Sometimes my reverie was pleasing, as though I had been reading a heroic romance. Other times it was troubled, for when I read romances, the characters might be Romans or Spaniards, yet they were always much like me. But the people Edward had been among did not seem like me in any way.

However, all those thoughts were yet to come. The first time I went into that room I knew only that I was uneasy; indeed, I stopped as suddenly upon its threshold as though I had bumped into a wall.

"What is wrong?" Edward asked. He had gone before me into the room, and set two tankards upon the little table there, where all the things needed for writing were already laid out: a dozen quills and a knife to cut them, an inkpot, paper, and a tray of sand. The fire burned bright, for it was yet February, and indeed, there had been frost on the street that very morning.

"I have been told many times never to go alone with a man into one of the inner rooms of a tavern," I said frankly.

He stared at me as though incredulous. "You cannot think—surely you do not fear—"

"It is not that. But if someone should see us through the window, and believe ill of me—that I would not like."

A quick, rueful smile touched his lips, and then was gone. "I did not think. I beg your pardon. English maids have so much more freedom than those in Algiers, I had forgot that there are still many rules and customs by which you must abide. We will sit where my mother has us both in good view, will that suffice? I had only thought to keep my story close until it is printed." He began to collect the writing things. "I will send the potboy back for the wine, that will be best," he said.

But by now I felt all the foolishness of a custom that would place us among the noise and vulgarity of the common rooms, and expose our work to many ears. I saw, too, that if I liked to keep what I did from my father, it would be better if we did our work privately. Edward was no stranger, after all, but a man well known to me, and to my family.

"No, let us remain here. You are right, 'tis better so."

He stopped in what he did, and looked at me. I advanced into the room, to show him that I meant what I said. "Are you certain?" he asked as I came near him.

"Very certain."

Then we sat at our table, and once more he spread the

writing things before me. We lifted our tankards and drank the King's health, and began at last to work.

"I have thought much about the start of our book," I said to him as he sharpened a quill for me. "We must begin by declaring the truth of all that will follow."

He was surprised. "Why must we do that?"

"So many kinds of tales are printed today that a reader may not know if he has before him a story of the fantastic or a serious history. So it is usual to declare at the start the truth of what has been written."

"But do not all accounts do this, whether they are fantastic or not?"

"Yes, almost all."

"Then how is the reader to know which are indeed true?"

"He must depend upon his wit for that. But people long to believe that the marvelous things they read of are indeed real, and they find comfort in such assurances."

Edward shook his head and handed me a quill. "I will leave such protestations to you. When you are done with them, you may report what I have told you; I assure you every word of it will be true."

"Then let us begin with how you were taken captive."

He stood then, and walked about the room, with his hands clasped together behind him. I thought of lions, which I had seen in the menagerie at the Tower, because of his beard and his yellow hair, and because there was an angry power in him as he paced from corner to corner. At last he came to his chair, opposite me, and stood with his hands upon the back of it. "I find I do not want to begin at the beginning," he said.

I thought for a moment. "It does not matter. I will arrange things in their proper order when the time comes. Where, then, shall we start?"

Now he sat, and wrapped his hand around his tankard.

"I will tell you something of the place—of the people. We say 'Turks' and 'Algerines' and 'Moors,' as though there were no difference. But there are many peoples on the Barbary Coast. There are the native people, that are called Berbers or Barbars. That is why we call their lands Barbary. They do not speak Arabic, but have their own tongues, several of them, depending upon where they are from, even as a Welshman speaks a different language than does a Scotsman."

"Edward. Your readers do not care about the Berber tongue."

Our dinner came just then, two courses: a dish of carp and a pasty of beef. Edward ate the fish hungrily, though he did not touch the pasty. As he ate he continued to speak of history in a voice that showed much enthusiasm for his subject. "The Arabs came many centuries ago, and brought with them the religion of Muhammad," he told me. "They were resisted, but they conquered at last, and in time the Berbers embraced Islam."

I was content to let him speak of ancient times while I attended to my dinner, but once the table had been cleared and I had my pen once more in hand I brought him back to the point.

"What of your captivity, Edward? What of Barbary pirates?"

"Ah, the pirates. The corsairs of Algiers have sailed the Mediterranean for generations. The Spanish, to defend themselves against piracy, established a fort on an island that looked upon the city. Algiers was at that time ruled by the pirate Barbarossa—surely you have heard of him? The name means 'red beard.' He appealed for help to the Ottoman Empire, for the Turks were also followers of Muhammad. In the present day, Algiers is an Ottoman province; Tunis and Tripoli, too, are part of that empire. Morocco, however, is not under Ottoman dominion, though its rulers practice their own piracy—"

"I suppose that your master in Algiers explained all this to you."

"Do not speak of my master." The command was quick and angry. "It is not yet time to speak of my master."

I laid my quill upon the table, wondering at the sudden change in him. He did not meet my gaze, but looked downward, into his cup.

"Did you not come to me because you had some trust in my art?" I asked him. "Because of what I know about putting pen to paper?"

"Yes, that is why."

"Then believe this: It is your experience, and not your knowledge, that has made you the fittest person to tell this story. You must relate to me what befell you. If you do not intend to do that, there is no use our spending this time together."

"I will have much to say of my experience, when the time comes. But are you not curious to know what stirs me to share it with every man that can read? No doubt you will not be satisfied unless your readers weep, but *I* will not be satisfied unless they learn."

I was taken aback. "Of course our narrative must edify."

"It must do more; it must instruct. There is great ignorance here in London about the place I have lately been. I wish to dispel a few misconceptions—is that an ignoble reason to tell a story?"

This, then, was the plan I had scented when he first proposed our project. I opened my mouth, intending to scold him for his foolishness. Did he think that people would flock to buy his narrative because they liked to have their misconceptions dispelled? But then I saw it would not do to debate with him about it. Instead, I resolved to lead him gently through the wilderness of storytelling, and trust that together we would find the right path.

"I do not speak of reasons," I said with great reasonableness. "But the languages spoken by the Berbers, that is dry as dust! If you would correct our misconceptions, tell me something of Muhammadan women—there is a mysterious subject."

At that he laughed aloud, a good, true laugh, as I had not heard from him since the day we danced together at Anne's house, before he sailed. "Women are always interested in one another," he said.

I did not know whether to be annoyed or abashed by

his laughter, for while it seemed to me that men are as interested in other men as women are in women, it was also true that I was very curious to know if he had met in his travels any Turkish maid—any Almira.

But before I could argue with him, he spoke again. "You must not say Muhammadan, for they do not worship Muhammad, as Christians do Christ. They believe that God spoke to the Prophet Muhammad, even as he had done to Abraham and Jesus."

"They believe in Jesus?"

"They believe that Jesus was a prophet. They do not believe He was divine. They say there is no God but God, and find the idea of the Trinity absurd."

"It is not absurd! It is most holy!"

"I will not argue that with you. But do not say 'Muhammadan,' say 'Muslim.' "

"Tell me something about Muslim women, then."

"I did not see a single Muslim woman in all my months in Algiers," he said. I looked up at him in astonishment, and saw that he jested with me. "I saw veiled creatures who *may* have been women, but I can offer you no evidence. I do not believe my master would have known his own wife if he had passed her in the street, the women are so concealed. And men who know each other quite well never set eyes on one another's wives."

"Did you—were you ever in a harem?"

"I have heard that a Muslim man may have more than one wife, but no man I met did so. I do not know how it is in the palaces, but in the houses of Algiers the women do not sit prettily in harems all day long. They are always working hard, grinding corn and baking bread, milking the cattle or preparing the meals—yet they are not permitted to sit at table with the men, nor to go to the mosque."

I was writing as fast as I could. "What is a mosque?"

"Why, that is where they worship, like our church. Oh, Meg, there is so much to tell you!"

"But first the women."

"How much would you like to hear?"

I did not need to look at his face to know that he bantered with me again, but I did not care. "Everything."

"Why, when a couple marry, the men must leave the feast as soon as they have had their fill, but the women tarry and send the bride into the wedding chamber. When the couple are at last alone, the bride removes her drawers, and puts them beneath her that they might receive the proof of her virginity. And when the couple have known each other as man and wife, the drawers are thrown out to the women who wait outside the chamber, and there is much singing and rejoicing, and the entire neighborhood will know if all is well. Do you blush, Meg?"

"No one who has been to the playhouse will blush at such a thing as that," I said. "And if all is not well?"

"Then the bride must expect to be divorced."

"I do not think such a custom would serve us here in England, where in some cases the groom himself has rushed the matter," I said. I had finished a page, and scattered sand across it as I spoke, that the ink might dry more quickly.

"Did I not say that English maids have more freedom than those of Algiers?"

"Do not think for that reason that we are wanton," I said sharply, for I did not like the way he spoke of English maids.

"Certainly I would not think it of *you*," he said, to soothe me.

"And how did you learn of these Algerine customs?" I asked him, which was what I most wanted to know.

But that question he would not answer. Instead he told me that there was no King of Algiers, as Englishmen believed, but that the city was ruled by a dey, who was a kind of governor sent from Constantinople by the Turkish Sultan there. I wrote it all down with a spirit of philosophy, hoping that the patience I practiced now would beget stranger revelations in the future.

～ 3 ～

I said nothing to Will about my meetings with Edward, not because I feared his jealousy, but because I was wary of his rattling tongue. I did not dare let any word of this business come to my father's ears before the work was finished. Perhaps, too, I did not want to hear again about the lesser pens of female authors.

But though *I* did not speak of Edward Gosse, Will hardly let a day go by without some sly mention of his name. Since I had told him plainly there was no cause for jealousy, I concluded it was only a part he liked to play. Perhaps it was a way of telling me that he cared for me, or it might be that it puffed him up to think that he could win me from a wealthier suitor.

But whether we spoke of Edward Gosse or of some other subject, the air between us seemed to dance. I remembered what Susannah had said, that there was no finer time for a maid than this, when she was not quite won and must be wooed, and I thought to myself that she was right. Will seemed to enjoy the dancing air as much as I. He spoke often of what he would do when he had his own shop, and jested about his future wife.

"When I have my own shop, the apprentices will not have to dust," he might say, as he drew his rag across the table. "My wife will do such work; that is what women are for." Or he might row in the opposite direction, saying, "When I have my own shop, my wife will not be bothered with such duties, but will spend all her afternoons at the theater, if she likes."

I gave his foolery back to him by speaking of my future husband: what fine table manners he would have, and how anxious he would be to solicit my opinion on all things. And in my head I kept a tally of how often I drove him to temper with my words, and how often to laughter.

Usually I took care to make sure our banter took place within doors, where a customer or perhaps my father might come upon us at any moment, for I knew that Will had read every word of *Mysteries of Love and Eloquence*, even as I had. On one occasion, however, this safeguard failed. The

shop was closed, for it was a hanging day, and people like
more to see an execution than to read about one. Will had
gone with the crowds, or so I thought. For myself, I stayed
at home and pondered the notes I had made for Edward's
narrative. We had met several times now at the Three Bells,
but our meetings had not gone well. He did not jest with
me as he had at our first meeting. He was often sullen, and
still he refused to put himself in the story but kept stubbornly to the customs of the Algerines. I looked doubtfully
at the many uninteresting things I had written down, and
wondered if our narrative would ever flower.

Father was not home for dinner that day, and Susannah
and Deb and I were very dull at table. Afterward I resolved
to take a walk, for March was half over and the weather was
beginning to warm. Will met me almost on the doorstep—
I knew not whether he had been awaiting me, or whether it
was mischievous fate that took a hand. We looked at one
another and then, without speaking, went together into
London's streets. Soon we were following the Oxford Road,
like everyone else; it was so much easier than to go another
way. Will bought some Dutch biscuits of a crier, and we
ate them as we walked until at last we drew near to Ty-
burn Tree, where counterfeiters and cutthroats were being
hanged. By then the road was filled with blossoms, strewn
by the girls who walked before the carts in which the con-
demned rode to their deaths.

"Come," Will urged, pulling at my arm, and we
pressed forward. We passed a woman who was selling gin-
gerbread, and another who had a basket of oranges, but we

did not buy. At the great scaffold a man stood in a cart, dressed in bright blue and yellow, as fine as though he went to his wedding instead of his death. There was a rope around his neck. My heart quickened as I watched, and then the hangman lashed his whip at the horse, which leaped forward, and the man hung kicking in the air—I put my hand to my mouth.

"You will not want his touch upon you, you are healthy enough without that," Will said, as people crowded close to put the dead man's hands upon their flesh, for the touch of a hanged man was said to heal. "Shall we see another?"

I shook my head.

"Then let us go the alehouse in Fleet Street; the executioner will come there later, and sell the rope. I will buy you an inch, if you like." And he led me away from the crowd before another hanging could begin.

I was breathless even now, and my blood seemed to dance within me. I think Will knew what I was feeling, for his arm stole round my waist, and I realized he was not wearing his gloves. To my shame, though I did not want an inch of rope, I wanted his fingers there upon my stays, and I let them linger a moment before I pushed his hand away.

"We have not had my father's consent," was all I said, and he did not try again, which was as well. I thought to myself that, as *Mysteries of Love and Eloquence* did not reveal that a maid will be breathless when she has seen a man hanged, it must be something that Will Barlow had learned through his own experience.

Seven

I had promised to visit Anne in Salisbury Court the following afternoon, and afterward to dine with Edward at
the Three Bells, but for once I did both these things unwill-
ingly, for I would rather have spent the hours in the shop,
with Will. My resentment made me hurry, which was as
well, for though the day was fine the wind was brisk. I
thought as I turned from Fleet Street that I would not be
sorry to be indoors again. However, a few steps from Anne's
I met with Edward, who had just left her. His face was
troubled, as it was so often now, but when he saw me he
said at once, "Meg! Will you walk with me a little before
you call on Anne? There is something I must say to you."

"Can it not wait until dinner?" I asked with dismay, for
I did not want to lengthen my time with him.

"Now is a better moment."

So I resigned myself to his company, and we walked together past the pink brick and tall battlements of Bridewell Prison, toward the steps that led down to the Thames. The tide was out, and the muddy bank was dotted with children scavenging for treasures the river might have left behind. The water was like a floor crowded with dancers: the canopies of the tilt-boats bowed and dipped to the wherries and barges as their oarsmen labored mightily. But what held my eye above all else was a great ship with many masts that rocked in her moorings as she waited for the tide.

"Where do you suppose she is bound?" I asked Edward.

He looked at the ship, and then at me. "Where would you most like to go?"

Though his question surprised me I did not have to look far for an answer. "Oh, anywhere! Venice perhaps, where the streets are made of water. Or China, where the women bind their feet to make them tiny, or India, where pepper comes from."

"I think she is bound for Venice," Edward said. "Shall I row you out to her, so that you might go, too?"

I laughed, and he laughed with me. The wind was blowing his loose hairs this way and that, and they gleamed in the sun.

"Not today," I answered him. "I've no time. I am busy writing an account of someone else's travels."

"Here I am talking idly of foreign lands, when you have so much to do!"

But I did not mind talking of foreign lands, and was almost sorry when he at last spoke his mind.

"I am troubled about Anne."

"Is she unwell?"

"Not unwell. Not yet. But she worries a great deal about how to please her husband."

I could not keep a smile from my face as I said, "Women should never worry about such trifles."

But Edward spoke soberly. "Not at their own peril, they should not. She is not taking all the care a breeding woman should, and does things which I fear are beyond her strength. I have urged her to be careful, but she pays me little heed, only saying my mother was always active at these times. But not every woman has my mother's luck when it comes to childbed."

"That is true enough," I said, thinking of my mother's death.

Edward guessed my thoughts. "Your own loss will make you persuasive with Anne," he said. "Will you plead with her to be more careful? Her happiness hangs on this child."

I knew that he spoke truly, and promised to do as he asked, though I thought that he worried overmuch—surely Anne would do nothing that might injure her unborn baby. Still, his concern showed how good a brother he was to her.

But when Anne met me at the door I discovered I had interrupted her in the task of making biscuits; her face was red with effort as she beat the eggs and sugar together with the rosewater.

"Fie, Anne, are you mad? You must ask your servant to do such things for you."

"She has gone to the market; who knows how long she will be? And Ralph asked especially for biscuits tonight."

"It would be better for *you* to go to the market and for *her* to make the biscuits."

"I cannot bear the street smells."

"Then Mr. Rushworth must go without."

At this she exclaimed, so I took the bowl from her and began to beat, and Anne settled into a chair nearby. While I worked I lectured her on taking more care. I reminded her of all the little brothers and sisters I had lost, telling her their names, and how old each of them would be today, and I was glad to see that as I talked she grew sober, and then fearful, and at last resolved. Finally I was satisfied, and allowed her to turn to another subject.

"How does Edward seem to you?" she asked me.

I almost laughed to find that she was as anxious about her brother as he was about her. But I was happy enough to rest a little from my work while I answered her. The recipe said to beat these ingredients for an hour before the flour was added, and I had been at the task half that time already, but the sugar was still coarse. My arm was aching, and I could not help thinking that housewifery was twice the work that writing was.

"He seems well," I replied, thinking of the way the wind had blown through his hair as we stood near the Thames.

Anne shifted in her chair and smoothed out the needle-work in her lap before she spoke. Her belly grew bigger every week, and she was seldom comfortable now. "He is not himself since his return," she said when she was settled.

"Many things have changed, and some of them forever," I said.

"Indeed. But that does not mean that *he* must change. I am as happy as I once was, though my father has died."

"You were not happy for many months," I said, which was only half my thought.

She guessed the other half, and set aside the needle to put a hand upon her belly. "Yes, it has taken this gift from God to make me laugh again, I know. Perhaps Edward, too, will laugh once he has a family."

"Do not look to me for that," I said, and began once more to beat the mixture in my bowl.

"No, I have despaired of you, but I am introducing him to all the young ladies I know. We may yet be lucky. In earnest, Meg, I think there *is* something you can do for Edward, while he is telling stories to you. I do not ask what he has said, but I think it is the cruelties he suffered in Algiers that have soured him, and I hope when he is free of them he will be glad again. I look to you as to a physician, you see, that must bleed him to heal him."

"What folly," I said, but I could not forget her words.

My arm still ached when I met Edward that day at the Three Bells. As usual, he awaited me near the bar, so that I need not walk unescorted through the inner rooms where men sat drinking and smoking, laughing too loudly or striking unwise bargains or giving away their secrets as the day wore on and the wine flowed.

As we settled down at our table he asked anxiously

about his sister, and I assured him that she had promised to be more careful. As I spoke a great burst of laughter came from the next room, nearly drowning out my words, and Edward frowned.

"They do not pay much heed to the fact that it is Lent," he said as we settled down at our work table. "The Muslims have a season that is something like unto Lent, you know. It is called Ramadan, and lasts for thirty days." He paused. "Why do you not write this down? Ramadan is a holy time for Muslims."

I picked up my pen, but did not write, for I was thinking of what Anne had said, and wondering how I might help him to speak of those things that yet bedeviled him, and kept him from peace—and those things readers would be most interested to know. Of course he did not want to talk about them! Of course it would be painful! But had he not come to me, at least in part, that he might do so?

"You were taken captive in June, were you not?" I asked him. "Was the day fine?"

He looked past me, to the picture of the ship that was set upon by a great monster. "I do not know that people need yet another account of danger and evildoing," he said. "It is more important that they learn the customs of far-away lands."

"You need not do one at the expense of the other. But, Edward, people will want to know of that moment that changed your life."

He did not answer, but his face was so hard and bitter that I faltered, and thought of asking him to tell me more about Ramadan instead. Indeed, when I spoke again, I was almost surprised to hear myself say a second time, "The day was fine?"

"It was fine." His voice did not even sound like his own.

"And you walked upon the deck?" I asked.

"I walked upon the deck."

"What were your thoughts?"

"Surely I need not share my thoughts with every man in London!"

"Share them with me, Edward. Tell me all that passed that day, and trust me to know what must be put in and kept out. You will read it before it is printed, you know, and we may quarrel then about what is said, if we must."

He got up and prowled the room, as he had done the first day we met.

I waited until his face was turned from me, and said a third time. "The day was fine?"

"The day was fine!" he said angrily. Then he continued, more calmly, "Indeed, I thought the sun too strong. It heated all it touched that day—the ship's railings, the cloth of my shirt. The wind was fresh and fair; we made good sail. I stood upon the quarterdeck and thought I could not bear the many long days to come before we reached London. All I wanted was to be home. I was bitter because the sun that shone on me would never again shine upon my father. I was miserable, there upon the deck, in the last hours of my life as a free man."

"Not the last, Edward," I said gently.

He did not mark me, but continued to pace as he talked. "While I stood there a fellow passenger, Mr. Hughes, came up to me, and began a conversation. I believe he meant to divert my thoughts, to cheer me. He was with the Levant Company, and we spoke together of its fortunes—of trade, commerce, the building of wealth. Of what else will two merchants speak? He traveled with a son named Christopher, who was twelve years of age.

"While we were talking we heard a cry from the mate, who was atop the masthead. I did not turn to look. I told myself it would be a school of porpoises or large fishes, which interest sailors greatly, as do all things of the sea. But a murmur went up among crew and passengers alike, and I knew it could not be fishes. Then Mr. Hughes went to see what had passed, and so at last I, too, went leeward, where the crowd gathered. I could see nothing yet, but the word went round that a sail had been seen.

"After that I could think only of piracy, and every man among us had the same thought. There was then a debate, as to whether we should flee or fight. The captain feared that we could not withstand them, and so we made all possible sail in the opposite direction. But they gained on us; indeed, soon we could see the masts of three ships. Two of them were Turkish men-of-war. A third, though we learned this only later, was their prize, a Dutch ship that had been bound for home with a cargo of figs and calicoes.

"They drew nearer and nearer to us, and when it was clear we could not outrun them our captain commanded that we take in our sails and wait, which we did. There was now a new debate, as to whether we should allow ourselves to be boarded without resistance, or whether we should give battle. Our captain resolved that we should fight. Christopher—the child—was in a fever of excitement, talking of how many Turks he would slay when they came near us. It sickened me to hear it. I walked up and down the deck, that I might escape his chatter."

The light that fell across my page dimmed at the same moment Edward's voice ceased, and I looked up to see that he now stood before the window, staring out into the little lane there.

I did not want to cajole him into speech yet again, so I waited, but he did not break his silence. At last I broke mine. "There was a fight?"

"There was a fight. Eight died. Mr. Hughes fell at the first volley. The child screamed and begged for my help."

"And you told him, 'An Englishman shows no fear,' " I said. I saw the story unfolding, saw Edward standing at the railing, Christopher sheltered by his arm, while behind him the mast toppled and the ship burned . . .

He turned at last, and looked at me in the manner of someone who has lost a treasure, and tries to pretend it does not matter. "It was not so."

"What, then?"

"I said to him, 'Be silent, damn you, and take what is coming!' "

I gasped. "You did not say that."

"I did." He came to the table again, threw himself into his chair, and gazed upon me in a way I did not understand.

I laid down my pen. "I will not put it in the book."

"Of course not. How could you? I knew that we would not tell the truth in our narrative, whatever our promises."

"True or not, it cannot be printed. You would not want it printed, Edward. Why did you say such a thing to a child?"

"Because there was no one there to say it to me."

I could not speak. Without thinking, I put a hand upon his arm. He did not stir; he seemed almost not to breathe. I knew not if it was because he could not bear my hand there, or because he treated it like a butterfly, which he did not wish to frighten away. All the while he kept his gaze upon me.

At last I lifted my hand and retrieved my pen. "Let us go on," I said, as though I were not shaken. "You were boarded?"

He took up his tankard and found it empty. "Boy!" he shouted into the next room. "We are thirsty here!" His voice was so great I would have held my ears if I had not held the quill instead. Then he said more quietly, "We were boarded. You will like this next. Who do you think was with the pirates?"

I cast wildly for a guess. "The Sultan himself?"

" 'Twas an Englishman, a renegade. He spoke to us in our own tongue—he scorned us. I will never hate an Algerine as much as I hate that man, may he rot—" but he stopped himself before the curse was finished. "I beg your pardon, madame," he said, as though he had never called me Meg. "I should not have asked you to hear this."

"But you did ask me," I said. "A renegade spoke to you in English?"

He nodded. "We were taken onto the Turkish ships, and put into the hold, and bound. But before we were put below, I heard the captain and the Englishman speaking together in Arabic. I could not make out all they said, but the pirates seemed well pleased with their prize. Our vessel carried bales of silk and a vast quantity of spices. I was in her hold once, and there was an entire room only of nutmegs; I stood in them up to my knees. I suppose it was because they liked their prize so well that they did not seek another, but resolved to return at once to Algiers."

The look upon his face changed when he said the name of that city where he had suffered in slavery, and I pitied him. "Shall we stop for today? I have already much to write about. We can speak another time of what happened next."

"As for what happened next, surely you know it," he said.

"That does not mean that you need not tell it."

"Why, I was sold, and for a good price, too, which pleased me. There was another man there of my class, a merchant named James Hill, from Bristol. The same man bought us both, but Mr. Hill did not fetch so high a price as I did, though I was a mere apprentice. Is not human vanity a strange thing, Meg? And it is a strange thing, too, to be asking always, 'What am I worth? Of what value?'

and to be speaking not of your accounts but of your very flesh.

"They opened my mouth—one buyer after another. They looked within and saw my teeth. I am missing only one; it was a matter for awe among them. Do you know, I have always been proud of my teeth, and taken great care with them, and yet, who has really looked at them? Before I left England, almost no one. But now a dozen men at least have studied them, and spoken together about them.

"Of course, it was not by my teeth that my price was determined. It was by my hands."

He held them out to me. Bewildered, I laid down my pen and took his hands in mine.

"Yes, you must feel them," he said. "Run your thumbs across the skin and feel its softness, search the palms for calluses, peer at my flesh to see if there are wrinkles. They are not the hands of a seaman or a carpenter. That is why it cost so much to redeem me."

I did not mean to do as he bid; how could I examine his hands as though I were buying a slave? And yet I *could* feel his skin under my thumbs, and with my fingers the palms of his hands. His flesh was warm, but it was not as soft as he believed, and I could feel the places his skin had thickened.

I turned my gaze from our hands to his face. He had closed his eyes.

"I am sorry the ransom was so high," I said. It sounded foolish, but I could think of no other thing to say.

He pulled his hands from mine. "You are like ice," he

said. "Come nearer to the fire. How do you write when your blood is so cold?"

He waited until I stood by the hearth, and my pen was far from me, to continue.

"When I heard how high it was set I grew faint," he said. "I was afraid it could not be raised. But Mr. Hill said to me, 'Of course it will be raised; why, all the merchants together will put in their pounds to ransom a man like yourself.' I chose to believe him, because I so greatly wanted it to prove true. But it was not true. I was not worth so much to the community as my captors hoped."

"It must have been a blow, when the ransom did not come."

"God has so many ways to teach us that we are nothing."

I did not know what to say, for it is true that we are nothing as compared with God, nothing to the vastness of the seas and skies. But that was not the nothing of which he spoke. "The merchants tried, Edward. They missed you sorely; they were outraged; they gave everything they could. They wanted to bring you home."

"Of course! They were anxious that I come to London, so I might collect the monies they would not give to my mother! You cannot imagine how happily I was greeted upon my return."

"They were fearful for their own fortunes, that is all. Sometimes when we are afraid, we do things we wish we had not."

Edward stood and pulled his gloves on. "I suppose that

is meant for me," he said angrily. "But you had better know that I regret nothing."

I did not want to leave him, for I had stirred the pond, and now the crayfish were angry and snapping. I feared someone's finger would bleed before Edward was calm again.

"We will speak more of this after dinner," I said.

"Not today. I cannot bear another beef pasty. I will stop at a cookshop on my way to the warehouse."

I could not persuade him, but left in great distress, and wondered if it were better to have left the pond alone.

🙢 2 🙢

We did not meet at the Three Bells again for more than a month. I had been seeing him twice each week, on the days that I came to Anne, but after that conversation he sent me a letter—by good fortune, no one saw it but Deb and me—to say he was much occupied with business just now, and that our next meeting must wait. I was sure that he lied, that he could not face telling me the things that remained to be told. But even if he had wanted to meet, for a little while *I* could not, for it was then that my father said sending the laundry out to be washed cost too much now that the family had grown, and we must wash our linens from now on at home. That was a task that required much labor. Betty rose at two of the clock to heat the water, and Deb at four to help her begin the washing. After a bit of oatcake in the morning the rest of us joined in: Susannah and myself and Joanna; even little Toby helped carry piles of linens to the buck tub, where they were put to soak in a lye Susannah made of wood ashes and urine. After the things were soaked they must be rinsed, of course, and soaked again, and rinsed again, until they were cleansed at last. Then we wrung them out and spread them upon the hedges that grew behind the shop, until the garden was white with sheets and shifts, smocks and petticoats, all drying in the sun. At last we smoothed them, using an iron that was kept warm by a lump of coal held in a hollow within.

We began on Monday, and when we finished Thursday night we were every one of us exhausted. Thank the Lord, we had so many linens that we would not need to wash again before midsummer.

Washing kept my arms busy that week, but not my thoughts. Even while I stirred the clothes in the tub my mind wandered to Edward's narrative, and I thought of one beginning after another to his story. Words came so readily that I nearly cried because I could not stop and write them down; I greatly feared that when at last I had the strength and freedom to reach for a quill they would be gone. And indeed, I found when the time came to write that some words had been lost. But some remained, and new ones, perhaps better, came when I made way for them.

A dozen different times I read the notes I had made when Edward spoke, and I wrote the scene out a half-dozen ways. Yet I was not satisfied. There were so many things to consider as I wielded my pen. What would please the readers who paid their shillings for a good tale, what would please the censor, what would please my father enough to send it to print, what would please Edward, who must read it first of all? And, too, I must consider how to please myself—or if not myself, that spirit that sat upon my shoulder as I wrote, urging me to speak of the sunlight on the sea, or the nutmegs in the hold.

Late in April I did see Edward, though it was not at the Three Bells. I received an invitation from Mr. Hodges, a merchant who was a friend of Susannah's family, to join a large supper party at his house, with cards and dancing afterward. He had two daughters near to my age—the older was named Sarah, and the younger, Peg—and there were several young men there who might be fine matches for them: Richard Hollingsworth, who had studied at Cambridge, and Gilbert Pierce, who was a goldsmith. And Edward.

When I entered the parlor he and Peg were standing together before a great globe that had upon it a map of the world. It was the finest thing of that kind I had ever seen, and at once I felt a pang, and wished we had it at the Star. Edward was pointing to a place on the globe, and laughing easily, and Peg answered back with something saucy, I guessed.

"You know him very well, do you not?" Sarah asked as she came to welcome me to her house.

I was cautious in my answer. "His sister Anne is my good friend."

"The business thrives now that he is back, so I have heard."

"I believe it does."

He did not speak to me until the evening was well advanced. He was not near me at supper, and after the healths were drunk those of my sex withdrew into another room, where we spoke of recent betrothals and the scandals of the theater, and those who wished to do so used the chamber pot. After a time we rejoined the young men for cards, but Edward played ombre at one table, while I played cribbage at another. At last there was dancing, however, and Edward came and bowed to me, and we stepped toward one another and then away, as the figure required.

"I'm glad to see you in light spirits," I said to him when the fiddler rested his bow. "The last time we met, I felt I was a barber who pulled out your teeth."

"My lovely teeth, that have been talked of by so many," he said with a laugh.

"When you have the time, I would like you to read what I have written as a consequence of that meeting."

"Must I? Must I think of such things tonight? I do not wish to, Meg. Do not make me." His face was flushed; he had drunk too much wine. For a moment I wished that I might forget myself as he did. But maids may not take the same liberties as youths.

"Are you speaking secrets here?" Peg asked us as she came near. "Tell all. Whose reputation do you ruin tonight?"

Edward did not like her words, and scowled. "None but my own," he said roughly.

"You are telling Meg your secrets, but you will not tell me?" she said, pouting.

She only meant to tease; there was laughter on her lips, and the pout was all pretend. But his good humor was gone. "My secrets need not concern you," he said, and turned away.

Peg colored, and her mouth was angry.

"He does not mean to be rude," I said. "He has not yet recovered from his ordeal."

"It is not your place to apologize for him," Peg said, and she left me.

The words stung, and yet I knew she was right. I reflected soberly that I had better not speak for Edward again, or people would think things that were not true.

➳ 3 ➳

If I had considered, I would have made long visits to Anne during those weeks that I did not meet with Edward. But as I did not, Will, who always noticed everything, remarked upon it one afternoon while we were in the shop.

"You do not spend so much time with Mrs. Rushworth as you once did," he said from behind the counter.

I looked up from Mr. Otway's play *Venice Preserv'd*, thinking that I did not get so much read now as I did before that day in St. James's Park. My father had not let me see the play when it was at the Duke's Theatre, and now that it had been published I was eager to find out why.

"One of her cousins from Surrey has been there much of late, and I am not wanted so greatly," I replied. This lie came easily to me, for Anne's cousin had indeed stayed with Mrs. Gosse in Broad Street for a fortnight, though she came to Anne's lodgings only once.

"It is well to have family about at such times. When my wife is with child, every cousin I have in the nation will come to visit her."

I closed my book and laid it on the table at which I sat. "Perhaps your wife may like some peace and quiet." My voice was weary, for that afternoon I was not in the mood for our game, but Will understood my tone differently.

"My wife shall have whatever is most necessary for her health and the health of her child, whether visitors or peace and quiet," he said earnestly. "She shall have the best midwives to attend her, or a man-midwife if she prefers, and need fear nothing when her time comes."

I knew that he was thinking of my mother's death, and I was moved. "No one can promise that," I said gently. "But we will not worry about such things now. We have much time before us."

"Mr. Gosse, I am pleased to see you looking so well!"

I turned, disbelieving, as though I would find that Will addressed the air, only in order to provoke me. But no, Edward stood by the door, which we had left propped open because the day was fine. I colored, angry at myself, for I knew that I had spoken as though Will and I were betrothed.

I could not tell if he had heard, however. He bowed, and approached me with a smile. "I hope you are well today," he said. "I came that I might read what you—what you recommended to me the other night."

It was my earnest gaze, the faint shake of my head, that stopped him mid-sentence and made him change course. I knew I must now think quickly, but Will spoke before I could. "Was it *Mysteries of Love and Eloquence?*" he asked, holding a copy of that work aloft.

"Certainly not," I said sharply. " 'Twas *The Life of the Valiant and Learned Sir Walter Raleigh.*" I snatched it up and handed it to Edward.

"A model for those of us who are less valiant and learned," Edward said, and felt obediently for his purse.

I hardly waited for his back to disappear into the street before I spoke angrily to Will. "What were you thinking? You will not bring our customers back by mocking them."

Will's smile was well satisfied. "You wish he had not overheard us, but he would have learned it sometime."

"Do not speak that way. Nothing is resolved. The settlement has not been proposed. The lawyers have drawn up no papers. You have not even spoken to my father!"

He no longer smiled. "Have you changed your mind, then, since he has returned from Algiers? Do you mean to marry Edward Gosse?"

"He has not asked me! Nor has anyone else," I pointed out. "At present I am without suitors."

"But if your heart is set upon him—"

"Do not be so foolish, Will."

"Am I foolish?"

"Very foolish."

This mollified him, which made me smile, for it is not often you can make a man happier by calling him foolish.

Eight

The next morning was the first of May, and the milk-maids came with fiddlers and danced a jig in the street while we crowded the window to watch them frisk and stamp. Susannah held Harry up so he could see, and Joanna held Eleanor by the leading-strings that trailed from the back of her coat so she would not go too near.

"Why do they dance?" Toby asked as he watched.

"It is the custom for the milkmaids to dance on May first," I answered.

As the music ended, my father came into the street and put some coins into the hand of one of the milkmaids, who curtsied her thanks.

"Why does he pay them?" Toby wanted to know.

"Because they bring the milk-ass to our door each morning, so that you and Eleanor can have something wholesome to drink."

Watching the milkmaids dance put me in good humor, but what pleased me even more was that before the morning was out a letter arrived from Anne—that is, the direction was written in her hand, but inside there was a note from Edward.

"Now that I have read about the noble sufferings of Sir Walter Raleigh, I hardly see the point of sharing my own pitiful adventures," he wrote. "However, if you should be inclined to continue work upon them, I will be at the Three Bells this afternoon after dinner. Please bring what you have written. I am sure it is worth more than the two shillings I paid for the edifying book about Sir Walter."

I went, of course.

"Has Mrs. Rushworth's cousin gone back to Surrey?" Will asked as I left, and I said she had, which was true.

I smiled my way through the streets, pausing now and then to admire the little blooming things that opened in the spring air, and when I heard a toyman crying his wares I hastened to catch him, and bought of him a whirligig for Toby to play with. Indeed, I played with it myself as I walked, whipping the stick through the air and watching the windmill sail in circles. At the steps to the Three Bells I hesitated, for I liked not to go into that place of gloom and smoke on such a fine day. But at last I did go in, for Edward awaited me there.

He was at the bar with his mother when I entered. He came quickly to my side and spoke in a low voice, as though we were highwaymen conspiring to rob a coach. "I did not know our meetings were so secret," he said. "That you wanted to surprise your father I remember, but I supposed he knew—I supposed that everyone knew, in general, what we were about. How have you explained your absences from home?"

And now my smile faded, for I saw that our meeting together would be most earnest—as, indeed, all our meetings were. I told him how I coupled my visits to Anne with the work we did on the narrative. "My deception has been more serious than you imagine," I confessed. "I do not hide this work from my father to please him, but because I am afraid."

At this he looked grave, and took me into the little room where we worked, and when we had seated ourselves before the fire I told him that my father had forbidden me ever to share my writing with others.

"So I have undertaken this work under false pretenses," I said. " 'Tis true I am hoping to change his mind, but if I do not succeed, you will have told your story in vain. I do not know if you think it is a greater sin to do this against my father's wishes, or to have deceived you in this way." I did not look at him as I spoke, but beyond him, to the window. A woman in a servant's white hood hurried through the passage. A splash of dark liquid rained down, the remains of a soup, perhaps, that was thrown from some higher window. Still he did not speak, and my hope began to fail. "Well, that is my story," I said. "I have our first chapter in my bag. Shall we put it into the flames?"

But he did not answer that question. "I think your greatest sin is that you have deceived Will Barlow," he said.

I was surprised, and looked at him closely, but he did not seem either angry or mocking. "You are betrothed to him, are you not? Or did I fail to understand you rightly when I was eavesdropping upon your conversation yesterday?"

He smiled a little as he spoke these words, but I did not smile in my turn. "Mr. Barlow cannot enter into any contract while he is bound to my father."

"Surely Mr. Moore would release him from that constraint."

"If he is to set up a business here in London, he will go much further if he has the freedom of the Stationers' Company, and for that he must serve the rest of his seven years. But, when the time is right, if all parties are agreed about the terms, then, yes, we will marry. He is a good man, Edward. I ought to have told you before now that he played a great part in raising your ransom, going from parish to parish, even as I did."

He had the look of one who has bitten into moldy bread, but he said, "I am grateful to him. I wish you both well."

I spoke in a guilty rush. "You will find your own chance at happiness soon. I am sure there is an English maid who is yearning for your heart, even now—"

"For God's sake, Meg, do not weave one of your tales around me!" he said sharply. It was as though he had struck me, speaking so scornfully of my "tales," and I drew back in my chair. He continued more quietly. "There is only one tale that holds my interest now. When I am of age, and the business thrives, there will be time enough to think about marriage, and look for a sensible bride whose dowry will help to secure the business. That is all I ever meant to do, you know."

I had been staring down at my bag, which held the unread work he had asked me to bring, and at my gloved fingers that clutched it so tightly, but when he said that, my chin went up, and I replied, "That is not what you wrote to Anne from Leghorn."

He looked displeased. "I do not think either of us should trust Anne with our secrets in the future; she has not done well by us. But believe me, if I was not a practical man before, I am one now."

"And I am practical as well. It is a great chance for me, Edward. I have never wanted anything except to be a bookseller."

"And to write. Does Mr. Barlow admire your work?"

"He has not seen it. He has no regard for female authors."

"You do not prefer a pastime of which your husband will approve?"

"Oh, we will be the sort of couple who always dispute; there are many such."

"You must ask Anne for her opinion on the happiness of a quarrelsome marriage." He pushed his chair back a little, and stretched his legs out toward the fire. When he spoke his voice was light. "I do not think it is well, Meg, that you meet in secret with a man who once sought to court you, to do something you are sure your future husband will not like. I confess, however, that I am not as shocked as I should be to hear of your lack of submission to the man you wish to marry, or even to your father, whose rights are indisputable. I fear that my time of servitude has somewhat altered my perspective on authority. I have not those feelings that every Englishman ought to have concerning King and commoner, father and son, husband and wife—or master and slave."

"You do not mean to challenge the King's supremacy!"

"I do not challenge anything. I have not come back to England to make challenges. But I see things differently: that I cannot help. The blacks pale, the whites darken; things are not as they were."

He was not looking at me now, and I eased the glove off my right hand, that I might seize from the table one of the quills that awaited me there and begin to record his words.

Then, abruptly, he turned the subject. "Margaret, this narrative you are composing—do you mean it to be the last thing that you write?"

"Of course not!"

"Will you write in secret all your married life, and burn your words in the grate that your husband may not find them?" I shook my head. "Then you had better tell Will Barlow about this work. That is my advice."

"I did not ask for your advice."

He was silent a moment, as though stung. In the quiet I heard the sound of dice against the wooden table in the next room. I realized that men were gaming there, and thanked God that my father did not know where I was.

At last Edward spoke. "No, you have not come to me for advice, have you? You have come for the story of my captivity; that is what you long to hear. You want to know of the humiliations I have undergone, and the abuses I have suffered. That is what will make you happy."

"Edward, stop."

"Stop? Why, we are just beginning. We had only got to the marketplace, where men put their fingers into my mouth, and turned my hands over in theirs, and felt my limbs to see if they were sound, and spoke over my head as though I were an animal. We stood there from early morning until midafternoon, while men came to gaze at us. Anyone can bid upon a slave, you know, Turk, Moor, Jew, or Christian. At last it was my turn to be sold. The crier praised me long, speaking of my youth, my soft hands, my learning, and especially my skill with foreign tongues. He spoke even of my comeliness. 'Look at this pretty boy, how beloved he must be,' he said. 'You can be assured that his father will pay a great ransom for him.' I wept when I heard him say it, for my father was dead, and could not pay a farthing, and I was afraid."

"Any man would weep under such circumstances."

"James Hill did not weep."

"His father had not lately died, perhaps."

He smiled a little at that. "No. His father had not lately died."

"What of the boy, Edward? What of Christopher Hughes?"

"He was sold that day, too. I used to see him, in later months, washing clothes at the shore of the bay. He is there still. He will grow to be a man in Algiers, and will become a Muslim and so win his freedom. He will take a Muslim wife, and live out his life eating figs and reading the Qur'an. Perhaps one day he, too, will buy slaves in the marketplace."

"That is a strange speech."

"Slavery leads to strange fates. It will not be all bad for him, you know. To the Turks a man's birthplace does not matter; a black African may rise to command others, or a white Englishman, as long as he follows the Prophet Muhammad."

"Tell me about your master."

"Yes, it will make you happy indeed to hear about my master. He was everything you have imagined him to be, I am sure. It was his custom to buy slaves in the marketplace when he thought a high ransom could be demanded. That day he bought only myself and Mr. Hill. Of course, he had household slaves to wait upon him, but I do not think he cared even for them. He did not like to be near us. He did not like infidels."

"*We*, the infidels!"

"Yes, of course."

"And you upbraided him when he called you infidel, and argued the merits of the Christian faith!"

"It was not so." For a moment he seemed almost glad to say this, but then he added, "James argued with him, only once. He spoke scornfully of Islam, and asked me to put his words into Arabic for him, which I did as best I could. Our master was enraged, and fell upon James with such blows that he was soon black and bloody. I tried to help him—"

"You pulled at the Turk from behind, but he was too strong," I suggested.

"I called out in Arabic, pleading ignorance and begging forgiveness, but every word inflamed him more. The fruit of my effort was that my master turned upon me and drew his knife from his belt, and came after me with it."

"Edward!" I did not look up as I exclaimed, but continued my hasty writing. I was thrilled to have uncovered such a drama.

"Yes. I would not be here now, except that—"

"You thundered in Arabic the one phrase he would listen to!" I guessed.

"His wife snatched at his arm."

"Oh!"

"She spoke rapidly to him—my Arabic was not yet good enough to understand her, but suddenly he dropped his arm, and then sheathed his knife."

"Muslim women, then, are not so different from Englishwomen, after all."

"Perhaps not."

He did not speak for a while, but my pen continued its scratching. I was using shorthand, and was not trying to put down every word he spoke, but even so I wrote as quickly as I could, and yet was always behind by the length of a sentence. When at last I was caught up, I said, "And afterward? Did you and Mr. Hill plot an escape?"

He looked at me in a strange way; I could not read his humor. Then he said, "When Mr. Hill and I spoke together afterward, he said to me, 'It was my pride and not my faith that prompted me to challenge our master, and God has used the Turk as His instrument to chastise me.' "

This took me aback, and I knew not what to say.

Edward shook his head. "It takes a deeper piety than I will ever know to see the hand of God in all things."

"Did your master put you to hard labor?"

"Hard enough, for a man who is not used to it."

"Did you row galleys?"

"Thank God, I did not. We worked at the limekilns. They are like great ovens in which the limestone is baked until only a powder of quicklime is left, the sort used for burials, and for many other things, of course. At first I stoked the fires, but I did not endure it as nobly as another man might. It is hot work, in June and July; again and again I fainted away. Mr. Hill was not so feeble. He roused me when I wilted, and gave me more than my share of water from the goatskin bottle. At last they put me to unloading blocks of limestone, which was toil enough. My hands bled and my muscles ached so much that each time I dropped a slab of stone, I thought to myself: It is the last, I cannot pick up another. And yet I did.

"Then Mr. Hill's ransom arrived. How sorry I was that he was redeemed with such speed!"

I looked at him quickly, to see if he meant what he

said. He was looking at me, and his face was filled with scorn, but I did not know to whom that scorn belonged, and almost felt he meant it for myself.

"He was sorry too—that was the sort of man he was. In his humility, he had been sure that I would be the first to be redeemed. It is *his* narrative that ought to be written down."

"He was released?"

"He was released, and I was left to deal with my master's anger that my ransom had not come as well." He had been staring at the wall, at the map of London there, but now he turned his gaze upon me, and it was wrathful, as though I were the one who had brought him to his suffering. "We are come to the part of the story that all readers want so much to hear. Of all adventures, it is the thing that interests us most. The *bastinadoes*. (The word is from the Spanish, of course.) Now, there is more than one way that the Turks administer this punishment, but this is how it was done with me. I was suspended from a staff, held by two strong fellows, with my head and shoulders resting upon the ground, and my ankles fastened in a loop of rope to the staff. Then a third man took a stick and began to beat the bare soles of my feet with it. I am sorry, I did not think to count the blows, I cannot tell you just how many there were; I am sure your readers would like to know that. And though our story would be nobler if I had not cried out, I *did* cry out, I screamed with pain—"

It was then that he saw that I was crying. He stopped his sentence, and did not begin another. In a moment, as

though he had just thought of it, he took out his handkerchief and offered it to me. I wiped my eyes, but it did me
little good, for they filled again at once.

"There," he said at last. "I have made you cry, which is
what I sought to do. That is the kind of fellow I have become."

At that I jumped to my feet, gathered my pages hastily
together, and turned to go. Edward seized my arm. "Meg—
I'm sorry. I beg your pardon. I should not have begun this
story, and I will not try to finish it. Do not come back, if
you please."

"No. I will not come back."

The moment he dropped my arm I fled, past the
gamesters, past a drunken man who tried to grab my skirt
as I hurried by, and then past a table full of men who
looked as vexed to see me as if I had interrupted them in
the midst of plotting treason against the King. When I
reached the common room Mrs. Gosse called out to me
from behind the bar. I did not heed her, but clattered down
the steps to the street, where I began to run, frightening the
hens from my path, and dodging a man bound for a tailor's
shop. Then I heard footsteps flying after me, and knew that
Edward tried to catch me, to strew more apologies beneath
my feet like flowers, no doubt, as I carried our narrative to
the scaffold. But I had the advantage of him, for he had
paused for thought before he acted, and did not have me in
his view. I left Cheapside and ran through a filthy lane,
holding my skirts clear of the turds and offal there. At the
end of it a great many crows were feasting on a heap of ref-

use; they scattered as I ran past, and I ran the faster because I was afraid of them. In this way I put one street after another between myself and Edward, until at last I realized that he had given up, and I could walk home without pursuit.

⟞ 2 ⟝

As I made my way through the darkening streets to our shop in Little Britain, I thought of Will as one thinks of a fire on a cold day. *Will* had never been captured by pirates, or beaten by Algerine brutes; he had never spoken a word of Arabic, and did not care what the Muslims believed. I longed to be with someone who gave blows and took them and the next day did not remember them, who caused no trouble week to week but caused plenty at Shrovetide or on Gunpowder Plot Day, when trouble was expected of him. I did not mind if he gave me orders, as long as he also made me laugh. And if he cared too little for poetry, what did that matter, as long as he cared enough for the prosperity of those who depended on him for their bread and board? In short, he was an Englishman in every bone and muscle, and that was what I longed for as I nearly flew through the open door of the shop.

Will's face gladdened at the sight of me. He dropped upon the counter the ledger he had been studying, and it shut with a clap. "You were long with Mrs. Rushworth today," he said.

For a moment I had forgotten all that I kept secret from him, and I felt I would burst from it. I remembered Edward's unwelcome advice, and saw now that it was sound. But Will spoke before I could.

"In the future do not be gone so long. It is burdensome on me, to do your tasks as well as mine."

I bit back sharp words, and began to move from shelf to shelf, straightening what was already straight. "How may I help you, now that I have come?"

"You have stayed away long enough so that I have done it all. When I am married, my wife will never leave our home without my consent." He wore a half smile now.

"When you are married, your wife will sneak away at all hours, for the pleasure of watching your face grow bright when she returns to you," I said, laughing.

He laughed himself, and blushed, but then he said, "Be serious, Meg. Wives must obey their husbands."

"And husbands must be reasonable in their commands."

He crossed the room to stand near me, so very close that I could feel the heat of his body, which was warmer than mine, as I had been long in the evening air. "I will always be reasonable," he said in a low voice.

"And you will not mind, will you, if your wife writes stories?"

But that displeased him. "It is not a wholesome use of time, for a woman."

"You think I use my time in ways that are not wholesome?" Somehow we had stepped back from one another, and the cool air blew between us.

"You are yet a maid. When a woman is married she forgets such nonsense; she has then other claims upon her time."

"Say clearly: Would you forbid your wife to write?"

He shrugged. "Of course I would not. Nor would I forbid her to go to the playhouse—unless by so doing she neglected her duty to her family. I am sure no woman I esteem could ever be guilty of such neglect."

His words ought to have dispelled my concern, yet I felt troubled as I considered them. However, before I could reply he said, "Do you not wish, Meg, that my apprenticeship was over, and I could put a signboard up tomorrow?"

"What is the good of wishing?"

"If I was to have a shop in Bristol, I would not need to finish my term. There it cannot harm me that I am not of the Stationers' Company. And my family are there. The competition in the book business is not so great. I cannot think of a better plan than to act sooner, rather than later, and open a shop in Bristol."

I looked at him with astonishment. "You are not serious. You cannot mean that you would be happy in Bristol after living in London."

"You have never been there. It is a flourishing port with fine shops and a very pleasing company of players. Let me speak to your father, Meg! I own, I am finding it harder and harder to think of waiting so long."

His appeal should have softened me, but it did not; indeed, I was angry that he understood me so little. "I will never live in Bristol! It has no wits who will idle hours away in your shop, there is no discourse there upon the great matters of Court and country. London is the center of the world, Will! You do not know how lucky you are to be here, at the sign of the Star!"

He did not answer for a moment. Finally he said, "You do not care for me. You toy with me."

"That does not follow."

"Do not mind what I said. It was a passing thought, that is all."

"I will speak to my father soon, Will. You are right in that; it is time for me to acquaint myself with his wishes. But I do not think he will want me to be hasty."

"Haste in business dealings is never good," he said, but I could not tell if he had chosen his words deliberately, or carelessly.

⇝ 3 ⇜

That night I read later than usual, for I was afraid to pinch out the candle, and to be alone with my own thoughts. But at last I could put it off no longer, and so lay on my back in the blackness, pushing idly against the bed curtain with one hand. I did not even try to sleep. Toby lay curled beside me, warming one hip, but as to the rest of me, I grew colder and colder. Even in the pit of me I felt a chill vacancy, like that which comes with dread. Then I

tried on one future and another, to see which was distress-
ing me: a bookshop in Bristol, for example, or speaking
with my father about his wishes for my marriage contract.
But what came to me were the words Edward had spoken:
Do not come back, if you please. And thinking of them, I
cried.

It was not the first time that I had labored with a pen
to no effect, certainly, but I could not recall any other occasion that had left me so cast down. For a few days I hardly
had life enough for the most ordinary of conversations, and
as for Will, I could not bear to be in the same room with
him, for though he said nothing, his countenance was
every day like a book, at one moment accusing me of a cold
heart, and at another asking when I would speak to my father, until I wished I had never learned to read the language
of faces. When my usual day came to visit Anne, he asked
me why I did not go, and I told him I was unwell. After
saying so, I found that indeed I *was* unwell: my eyes hurt
when I read, and my skin was hot, and my throat ached so
that I could hardly swallow. I told Susannah my symptoms,
and was sent to bed at once. There I penned a note to
Anne, apologizing for my absence. Then for three days I
was ill, and knew not if I would live or die.

I slept much, and when I did not sleep, it was very
much the same, for I saw the world around me as though
through a dream. Susannah was nearly always there when I
woke, and fed me spoon-meats, though I did not want
them. My father called a physician who asked me if I had
been lately near the Fleet Ditch, for a miasma of foul air

was said to hang about the river there. I shook my head weakly and closed my eyes again. They bled me, of course, hoping to restore the balance of my humors.

If the good doctor could not guess the cause of my fever, certainly I cannot tell it. All the same, I know what it was that worsened my headache and weakened my will. It was the thought of the narrative. Not because I had written words no one would read—that was often the case. Not because the work had come to an abrupt end; I had abandoned work half done many times before. But I was like the flea that drinks the blood of a dog, and now I was bloated from my feast. I had tried to suck Edward's story from him, that I might profit by it—no, worse, I had tried to suck from him a tale that was not in him, of things he had not done and feelings he had not felt. There was a wrongness in what I had written that spread from the words as contagion spreads from foul air. Thank God, Edward had never read it; thank God, no one had.

Toward the end of the fourth day of my illness it was clear I would not die, and on the fifth day I felt so well that I began to forgive myself. Certainly it was my fault that I had tried to make Edward tell a story that never happened. But it was not my fault that people liked more to read of pirates and slavery than of the native languages of far-off tribes, or the customs of strange religions. Broadsides about rogues and impostors were more popular than treatises about philosophy or alchemy, and accounts of executions would surely always be the most popular of all.

While I lay pondering these things, Deb brought me

notes to read in bed: two from Anne, one from Mr. Winter, one from Will—one from Edward. Anne's first was playful; she accused me of feigning my illness, and said she did not choose to give up my friendship simply because her brother had not the courage to tell his story to the end. Her next was full of alarm, for she had sent her servant for news of me, and found that I was indeed sick. Mr. Winter's was only a kind word. Will's was sweet: "I have heard that walks in London gardens are recommended for convalescents who have suffered your ailment; I undertake to assist you with this cure." I smiled at it, and put it beneath my pillow to read again later on.

Edward's note I put by, as though I would not read it, but then I could not help myself, and broke open the seal after all. He wrote: "Please God I bear no part in this cursed illness of yours. When you are well again—God willing—I pray you will meet with me *only once more*, that I might better explain my conduct."

I threw it angrily down upon the bed. What was the point in meeting *once more*, and never again? Why meet for apologies, if the narrative was never to be written?

I took up my quill and replied: "No explanation can be necessary. You wrong me when you suppose I do not understand." I signed it with my full name, and felt so much satisfaction that it effected my cure. By the next day I was out of bed, and the day after that, I sat at my father's writing desk in the parlor, wrapped in a woolen blanket, and began to tell again the story of Edward's captivity. I began it on a clean page, with a fresh word; I did not intend to pirate even a little from what I had done before. But after a time I did pick up the first work, and saw that although there was much that was bad, there were little things throughout that were pretty or useful. I worked late into the night on the new narrative, until my head ached and my eyes burned and the candles in the sconce had burnt to stubs. I ought not to have done so, having been so lately ill. But the truth was that I felt better for having written it, even though I could not see how any eyes but mine would ever read it.

The next day I helped my father in the shop while Will was at the printer. It was just the sort of day I liked, for we had customers enough, but none in a hurry. Among them was Mr. Randolph, who loved to talk of the theater; he told my father that an actress who had been said to be with child was not, after all, and bought two plays and a volume of poetry before he left. Mr. Newton, of the Royal Society, spent an hour looking into books on divinity, sometimes wagging his head yes and sometimes shaking it no, then Mr. Boyle arrived and the two of them took a glass of wine with my father, after which they left together without having spent a farthing. Soon after a man came in and bought a book for the girl he courted. At first he did not know what to bring her, being certain only that she could read, but after I had asked a few questions about her slippers and gloves I was able to discover that she cared more for home than for art or fashion, and sent him away with a very proper book of remedies.

Then it was quiet for a little, and, thinking of the man

who was courting, I determined that I would speak to my father about marriage, as I had promised Will I would do.

I started my sentence twice over but could not bring forth the words; it seemed I had at last been graced with the modesty I so often lacked.

"What is it, Daughter, speak!" my father commanded, looking up from the volume he had open upon the counter before him. "Or a customer will come, and your chance will be lost."

"I seek your counsel, sir, upon a matter of importance."

"What, then?"

I laid my dustrag upon the hearth and drew a deep breath. "It is time for you to make your wishes known to me, so far as my future is concerned."

He was surprised. "Why, Meg, you are meant to marry, you have known that always. It is why you are provided with a dowry."

"And what sort of man do you seek for my husband?"

At that he looked wary. "Is someone courting you, Meg? If so, you must send him to me."

I hesitated. Will and I had been careful not to say or do anything that would be called courtship before a magistrate, but that did not mean he was not wooing. "No one courts me now," I said at length. "But there are a dozen ways a maid may encourage or discourage a man who comes near her, long before he prosecutes his suit. I want to please you, Father."

He looked pleased indeed at this speech. "I welcome the suit of any man who may provide you with happiness and security. He must be a man of good character, of course—a careful man, not profligate or extravagant, a man who looks to his future. He must be prepared, both morally and financially, for the responsibility of a family." He paused a moment, then ventured a little further. "Susannah says always that you would be most happy with a bookseller."

"Is it your wish—do you think of Will Barlow?"

"Does he please you, Meg? Can you love him?"

I paused before speaking. I was standing by a little table covered with pages stitched but not bound: sermons and almanacs and the repentant words of criminals lately hanged. I looked from one stack to another as though I would find my answer among them, but I did not, and at last I looked again at my father. "How can I say? Certainly I am fond of Will. But, Father, not every match need be a love match."

"No, indeed, and I am glad to hear you speak so prudently. But once you are wed, it will be your duty to love your husband, and to seek to please him in all things. Is Will a man that you can learn to love?"

I did not answer. How can a girl know which man she will someday love? I remembered what Susannah had said about asking questions, but Will had not been married before. I knew of no one from whom I could discover how often he might strike a woman whose tongue was pert, or whether, like my father, he would be a man who could be gotten round by those he loved.

"You must think seriously on this subject," my father

said. "Consult your heart, but do not neglect your judgment. I have been married twice, and twice have had good fortune. I wish that you may have my luck in love."

Again I did not answer. I used my fingertip to brush a speck of soot from the stack of pages nearest me, feeling much troubled.

"There is no hurry, you know. You need not marry young, if you do not like."

Now I looked at him squarely. "But did not the amount of my dowry change when Harry was born?"

I could tell from his face that this had struck the mark, but he spoke sternly. "It is yet a fine dowry, Margaret, and will remain so. If you like to marry soon, the money will be there, if the bridegroom is suitable. But haste is seldom a friend to a bride. What man is it that you think to encourage, or discourage, with your arts?"

"I think of Will," I told him.

He smiled, and I saw that my answer had pleased him. "Then there is no hurry, for there can be no courtship until his term is served. Think of other things, Daughter; your time has not yet come."

Think of other things, my father had said, but instead I lay in bed that night and considered his earlier advice. *Consult your heart, but do not neglect your judgment.* Of course I would not neglect my judgment. I knew of three maids who had married for love against the advice of their families. Agnes Lane had married a man with few prospects, and now lived in poverty; her father and brothers would not see her, and only her mother pitied her. Mary Rodway had married a man of rank, though her father was but a freeman of the Clockmakers' Company. Her parents did not like the inequality of the match, and with good reason, for now Mary was ill treated by her husband's family and was most unhappy. I had not heard what had happened to Ellen Powell, who had run away with a man nobody knew, but I did not think it could be good, for now no one would speak of her. No, I would not neglect my judgment.

But my father had also counseled me to consult my heart, and to do so was no easy matter. When I pictured myself with Will at a stall in St. Paul's Churchyard, or at a bookshop in Westminster Hall—then, indeed, my heart overflowed with happiness. But when I imagined the two of us running a shop in Bristol I could not rejoice, and this sobered me. Marriage was no daydream, after all. If I married Will it would not be all reading plays and dining with authors. I must hire his servants, manage his household— bear his children. At this thought I grew unquiet; I turned over, so that I faced the bed curtains. I knew so much and so little of married love. Everything that could be read in a bawdy play or a book on midwifery, everything that could be overheard at night or glimpsed upon the stairs—that I knew. But how it felt to have warm and eager hands sliding beneath my shift on a cold night—that I knew not. Would it someday be Will's hands that touched me where no one had, his face that I glimpsed in candlelight? The memory came to me unbidden of the day I sat in the Three Bells with Edward and held his hands in mine—the hands that had been altered forever by what had befallen him. If *he* had been a bookseller—but that was like saying, I would love Thomas dearly, if only his nose were like John's.

Will was clever, and funny, and not ill-looking, and he cared for me. Surely in time I could learn to love him.

Nine

"How shall you call the child, if it is a boy?" I asked Anne as we sat in her parlor one afternoon in the middle of May. She was embroidering a bearing cloth of white silk, to be used at the christening, and I had work in my lap as well, a pillow slip that was meant to be part of my dowry. I knew that it would never be done, for I paused whenever I talked, and whenever I listened, and we were silent very little. Even when I seemed to progress, I did not, for I made many wrong stitches, yet I would not go back to pick out the mistaken threads. Instead I sewed hastily on, as though no one would ever notice. How different it was from my writing! There I went willingly over every sentence many times, and picked out not only those words that lacked luster among their fellows, but those threads that ran on to wrong places.

Yet I would have felt strange without work in my lap,

and so I forced my needle every now and then through the cloth, and cast envious glances at the shining threads Anne wove so skillfully into her picture.

"Mr. Rushworth and I are not agreed upon that subject," Anne said in answer to my question. "He wants to call his son after Mr. Wheatcroft, for whom he clerks, but I do not care for the name Francis. I want him to be called Philip, after my father, and to see that name handed down within the family."

"Surely Mr. Rushworth understands your feelings."

"He says that it is for Edward's first son to be so called, or Henry's."

"There is some justice there."

"You must not take his side against me," she said.

Though she smiled, I could see that she was in earnest, and I remembered Edward's words about quarrelsome couples. "Do you often have disputes?" I asked.

"Every day is not often, is it?" she said, still pretending to make a jest of it.

"Every day! Oh, Anne!"

" 'Tis not my fault, Meg. There is no pleasing him. What deceivers men are when they woo, all smiles and gifts and courtesies. What do we learn of them, really, until we are bound to them for the rest of our lives? And when I am made to submit to him in every small thing, soon I begin to argue about matters on which I don't even have an opinion! I am only glad my father did not live to see me so unhappy." Her voice broke, and she threw down her work and sobbed.

I knelt by her chair and embraced her, and when she quieted, I put my hand upon her pregnant belly and said, "You will not always feel so woeful."

"I hope you are right. He will be happier when he has an heir, will he not? Oh, may it please God to make this child a boy, and let us call him Francis if my husband so wills it, or Alphonse or Athelred or Canute, just so long as it is a boy!" And she began to sob again.

"You must not, Anne! You will harm your child," I said to her, but she continued to cry.

In the end I put her to bed, and made her a syrup of tansy and sage. "You must sleep now," I said as I took away her empty cup.

"But you will not go yet?"

"No, no, I will stay until the servant comes. But I will not speak with you, for you must rest. Have you a book that I might look into?" I asked without much hope, for Anne was not a great reader.

"There is a volume of Edward's in the parlor, that he left when he was here last. I don't know if it will interest you; it is in Latin."

I tucked the covers round her, and petted her brow, and went into the parlor to get Edward's book, wondering if I remembered enough Latin to make it out. It was a fine volume, with a gilded cover and marbled leaves; we sold few things as fine at the sign of the Star. I looked upon the first page to discover what it was that he treasured so greatly, and saw there, in large letters, the name of Catullus. These, then, were the love poems he had spoken of the day he came to see me, before he sailed for Leghorn. With great curiosity, I turned the pages before me.

Da mi basia mille . . . that meant *give me a thousand kisses.* And from another page I translated slowly: *You ask how many kisses would leave me sated . . . as many as are numbered in the Libyan sands . . .*

I confess I was surprised, and flattered, too. I remembered supposing that the amorous verses of Roman poets could only be dull, like the speeches of Cicero. But they were not. I could not help wondering if Edward still dreamed of many kisses between us.

On another page he had translated a line or two himself, writing in the margin: *Do not pursue her who flees, nor live miserably, but be resolved, endure, and be steadfast.* Again I was startled. Did he think of me, when he wrote those words? I was sure it was not Peg Hodges who was in his mind. I wondered when he had made these notes. Anne said that he had left the book behind when last there—was it before the day I ran crying from the Three Bells, or was it since? Did he love me still? If I no longer cared to be a bookseller—if I no longer fled—would he then come courting again?

I knew that I should close the book and set it down, or at the very most should occupy myself in translating one of the longer poems that bore no private markings. Yet I felt an eager tumult within, and turned the pages quickly until I saw his hand again.

Odi et amo, the poem began. And Edward had translated the whole of it in the margin. *I hate her and I love her.*

Why do I thus? you may ask. / I do not know, but so I feel, and it is like torture.

The door opened, and I started, so that I nearly dropped the volume, but it was only Anne's servant. I set the book carefully down exactly where I had found it, but I felt such agitation it was like pain. *I hate her and I love her.* It was not a good translation, for the Latin words did not reveal the object of such passion. The poet had written only: *I hate and I love.* Edward had added the pronoun. And this time I did not doubt that he thought of me.

It was not so surprising. Had I not asked him to hate himself, because he had not been the noble, fearless hero of a storybook? It was easy enough to forgive myself in my bedchamber, while yet nursing a grievance against Edward because he had brought our narrative to a close. 'Twas harder to do so when I had looked upon his written words: *I hate her.*

I went to Anne's chamber. She was not asleep, but lay quietly upon her pillows.

"I am sorry I was so foolish," she said at once as I entered. "I am better now."

"That makes me glad," I said with feigned good cheer, and took her hand.

"I am thankful you do not stay away from me because you are angry with my brother," she said.

"I am not angry with him."

"He has written you three times!"

He hates me and he loves me, and it is like torture. Or— it excruciates him? The Latin word was *excrucior*, which made me think of the martyrs.

"I believe I have answered him three times with courtesy," I said to Anne.

"But you will not see him, as he asks."

"It is better so. What can he say to me, Anne, that will be news?"

"There is no telling. In such discourse there is always the chance of a surprise."

"My life is not so dull that I seek surprises."

"Then you will never see him again?"

"Don't be foolish, we will see each other often, at dinners, and suppers—and here, very likely. I have told you that I am not angry."

"But you will never *meet* with him again?"

I looked at her, and saw that she was not asking from her own curiosity, but on Edward's behalf. Edward, who hated me. If I had anything in me of humility I would have said simply, "I will not meet with him." But I have known little of that virtue in my life, and could not help believing that, if only he would give me one more chance, I could unmake his hatred.

"If he likes to take up the work of telling his narrative again, I will meet with him," I said, and I knew that I had sent him a message, as clearly as though I had written to him.

The next afternoon I received a letter. The direction was in Anne's hand, but before I opened it I knew it was from her brother, and I knew what he had written me to ask.

∽ 2 ∼

Because Will watched me so closely, I did not dare to absent myself from the shop for an entire afternoon. Instead I sent a note to Salisbury Court saying that I would be at the Three Bells after church on Sunday. That time was my own, and I might spend it as I liked.

When I parted from the family at St. Botolph, I told my father I was going to Anne's. He took little notice, but I could see Will did not like it. I told myself that these meetings would soon be over, and then I would explain them to Will and he would laugh at me, and forgive me, and be content once more. It is the kind of thing you tell yourself when you are doing what you know to be wrong.

"Why, Meg, I did not think your father liked you to be at a tavern on Sunday," Mrs. Gosse said as I entered the Three Bells.

"He does not," I agreed. "Unless I have a very particular reason."

Edward's glance was sober as we greeted one another, but I saw nothing in him of hate or of love. I settled myself in the chair that faced the window, with my back to the fire.

"So you have changed your mind, and would like to finish your story," I said.

"I would." He looked at me and then past me, into the fire. "I always meant to tell it in full. But I did not know it would be so hard. Meg, I must beg your pardon, there is no excuse for the things I said when we last met. 'Twas not your fault—your fault that . . ."

"Of course it was," I said quickly. I tugged at my gloves, and kept my eyes upon the task as I spoke, for I did not know how he would receive my words. "I am so angry with myself! What was the good of your going far from home, and keeping your eyes and ears open, and suffering things you would not have had to suffer here, only to tell them to someone who will not hear the truth?" At last I made myself face him, though I knew my cheeks were warm. "Let us go on in a different spirit. You may speak of anything you like, and I will write down what you say."

"But, Meg, you have done nothing I did not ask you to do. I wanted my story told, I wanted you to tell it. And then—I wanted to hurt you with it, because of—because the telling was too hard."

"The thing that hurt the most you have undone, now that you are willing to finish your story." I opened my bag and took from it a clean paper, which I spread carefully upon the table, avoiding the deep marks there, that my quill might not puncture the paper by falling into those old grooves.

We began where we had stopped before. "It was after you received the *bastinadoes* that you wrote to your mother?" I asked him.

"Yes. I was made to write, though I was not told what to say. My master knew what I would want to say, after such a beating."

"And then what passed?"

"He did not even wait for an answer. I don't know why, unless it was a whim, or he had another opportunity. In any case, as soon as my wounds had healed a little he took me to market, and there I was sold again, to another Algerine."

Suddenly I remembered the anger in his voice when he said, *It is not yet time to speak of my master,* and was sure it was *this* master whose memory he had wanted to keep to himself.

"My life was easier at once. I did not work at the limekilns anymore, for my new master—his name was Omar—had bought me because I knew several tongues, and he wanted my help with translation. Not all slaves are put to hard labor, you know. Those who have a useful skill are often asked to employ it; carpenters are set to building, for example, and those who know something of munitions are welcomed with delight.

"I ought to have been grateful for my easier life, but I was not. With my first master I had not even freedom enough to be angry, but now I had, and for a time I made use of that freedom. I did poorly the work I was given to do, and when my work was done I flocked with other Christian slaves who spent their time idly. On a good day I played at quoits, or laughed at jests I'd heard a thousand times before. On a bad day I drank until I passed out in the street, or gamed away the little money I had."

He was silent for a moment, and I looked up from my page. He, too, had been staring down, but now lifted his eyes to meet mine.

"There were many bad days, Meg. I wish I could tell you something different." He smiled a little, and spoke in a voice that half mocked the stories I had read so often. "I wish I could tell you that I saved young Christopher from slavery, that I bested the infidel in debates about religion, that I defied my captors, took my blows unflinching, cleaved unto my Christian faith, and lived upright through all travails. But it was not so."

"Of course it was not," I said, as though I had known it always.

"If I had been another sort of man—"

"The sort *I* have had the pleasure to know. The sort that lives upon the printed page, and in no other place."

"That is not true. James Hill would never have spent his days gaming and drinking."

"Only God knows what James Hill would do in the most extreme circumstances. You are too severe upon yourself, Edward. You must be like me, and invent excuses for all your choices, and forgive yourself for your lapses. Only think, I am not beaten and enslaved and in fear for my life, yet I cannot do so simple a thing as to tell the truth to my father. Instead I say to myself: Now is too hard a time for truth! Later, when I am a woman grown, and have left my father's house, I will tell the truth always."

"To Mr. Barlow you will never lie," he said with a little smile.

I did not bother to blush. "Yes, that is what I say to myself. I do not suggest you go so far as that, but you may certainly allow something for circumstances. William Okeley, who was enslaved in Algiers and has written his narrative before you, did as much, and he is a deeply religious man."

"Did he so?"

" 'When the body is a slave, the reason must not expect to be free; and where the whole outward man is in bondage, the tongue must not plead exemption.' "

"Those are his words?"

"They are."

He said nothing more, but I thought he was not so oppressed in spirits as he had been, and I hoped that he would forgive himself, after all, and perhaps, someday, would forgive me as well.

~~ 3 ~~

We met too long that day. We talked until dinnertime, fortified ourselves with some lobsters and a fricassee of rabbit, and talked some more. We heard the bells ring to call people to the second service. The tavern emptied, and was closed, that the public might not enter, but we talked on. And when the time of the second service was past, and the tavern doors were flung open once more, why, still we talked.

"Omar was a merchant who did business with Christians, and Jews, too," Edward told me. "Of course they all used the lingua franca of that region—the trade language, you know. But there are often subtler matters to discuss that such a language does not encompass. He gave me work to do, he gave me something to think about besides England and freedom.

"When he bought me he had several urgent matters that required a translator, but when they were done he knew there would be no more work of that sort for some time. So he proposed that I begin a business of my own, and pay him something from my profits every week. This is a common arrangement in Algiers; they even have a word for a slave who has his own business: *ma'dhun*. If the master is a mean man, he will ask for so much that a slave can barely make enough to pay it. But it is not so with all masters. There was one slave among us who kept so much money from his business that, in time, he paid off his own ransom. However, he did not go home again—he stayed in Algiers and continued his enterprise, because it did so well.

"And so, with the help of my master, who put forward some capital, I set up in business, doing what I know how to do well. I ran a tavern. Muslims do not drink—that is, they are not supposed to drink, they are never to touch a drop of alcohol. But there are many others in Algiers who are eager to drain a flagon of wine—and there are also bad Muslims, as there are bad Christians. Mine was not the first tavern in Algiers; there are many such. But mine prospered, and I had soon repaid what my master had loaned me."

He paused, and drank from his tankard. When he set it down he said, "One night in the tavern a man who was a Christian and a slave came in but did not want wine to drink. He waited until I had a quiet moment, and then whispered to me that he had a plan to escape Algiers. That is not an easy thing to do, for the city walls are well guarded, and though a slave may go a little way outside the wall on business—to wash clothing in the sea, for instance—we were kept under strict watch. But this man asked if I was interested in knowing more of his plan. He said that I could be useful to him. I told him I would think about it, and to come back in a few days.

"In the night the sirocco came—have you heard of this? It is a dry, hot wind that blows over the desert from time to time, and brings great uneasiness with it. The sand flies until a man's clothing is filled with grit and he must walk with his eyes closed. When the sirocco comes, there are sudden quarrels, men fight with knives, animals break their tethers, leaves fling themselves from the trees as though in despair.

"All the while the wind was blowing, I could not bear it. Every small thing fretted me, until at last I resolved that I would join with the man who planned to escape, and flee this detestable land, even if my effort ended in death." He smiled. "It was my one moment of courage."

"It was your one moment of imprudence," I said. "You might be dead even now! But you did not keep to your resolve?"

"As you see." He was silent a moment, then said, "It was Omar who prevented me."

"He did not discover your plan!"

"There is no way that he could have known it, and yet he seemed to. One day at table, when we had finished our *couscous*—"

"What is that?"

"Why, it is crushed wheat steamed over broth, and served with meat or fruit and many spices. I ate it nearly every day, when I was with Omar."

"I should not have interrupted. You had finished your meal?"

"And Omar said, 'Come, let us sit in the courtyard for a little, and talk.' The houses in Algiers are beautiful, Meg, all built in the same style, around a courtyard, with a gallery upon the roof supported by pillars. That day the courtyard gave us some relief from the blowing of the wind.

" 'It is your first sirocco,' Omar said to me, and I said that it was. He said, 'In the sirocco, things done at night are often regretted in the morning. It is not a time to make changes.' I went cold with fear, thinking I had been betrayed by the Christian who had spoken of escape. Then he said, 'When the sirocco blows, it is easy to think that things cannot be borne—injury, or poverty, or dishonor, or slavery, or life itself. But it passes, my friend. The wind passes, and men find they can bear many things they believed they could not. And in time, those things, too, will pass. You will not be a slave forever.'

"He spoke to me so gently, Meg! At that moment his gentleness seemed like the thing I could not bear, for it reminded me of my father—he was my father's age. Then he said to me, 'Promise me that tomorrow afternoon you will sit here in the courtyard with me, and eat dates from a bowl.' I promised him easily, for I did not think any plan to escape could be perfected in so short a time. But when I had pledged myself, he said, 'And promise that when the sirocco has passed, you will come one night up to the rooftop with me, and look at the stars.' So I promised him that, too, thinking it would not hold me long in Algiers to honor such a promise.

"When the man returned to the tavern the sirocco had stopped blowing. I had eaten dates in the courtyard with Omar, but we had not yet been to the rooftop to look at the stars. That did not matter, for the man was not thinking of leaving for another week, at least. But I told him I would not join him. I told him my hopes of being ransomed were still high, and I would not risk them for his sake. In truth, however, I had been moved by my master's kindness, and did not want to injure him. Or perhaps I deceive myself—perhaps I was only afraid. A nobler man would have escaped, would he not, Meg?" he asked me with a smile.

"Then you had despaired of being ransomed?" I asked.

"I hoped on some days. I hoped on days that letters came, before they were read. On other days I did not dare to hope."

"And did you ever see the stars from the rooftop?"

"I did. Omar was a learned man, with a great interest in the heavens. He taught me the Arab names for the stars and constellations. They are different over Algiers than over London, you know. Not vastly different—the city is above the celestial equator by some degrees—but a little different. There are even a few nights on which you can see Canopus, which the Arabs call *Suhel,* 'the Plain.' It is almost the brightest star in the sky, and serves as a kind of polestar of southern climes that guides travelers through the desert.

And at some seasons I could see much of Argo Navis, the great ship that sails across the sky. Some call it Noah's Ark, and the Arabs name it *al sariuah*, 'the Ship.' But many say it is the *Argo*, that Jason sailed on to seek the Golden Fleece. Do you know that story of the Greeks, Meg?"

"Yes." Madame Clarke had told me the story of Jason's quest, and all the dangers he and his crew confronted on their journey to and from a distant land: giants, monsters, clashing rocks, singing sirens, an enchantress, and many other perils besides. I did not remember every detail, but it seemed to me that most of the characters died horrible deaths before the tale was over, as always seemed to happen among those unlucky people.

"One night in especial it was displayed—I saw its sail, and its stern, and its compass. You cannot see the keel unless you are farther south. The night I speak of— Put down your pen, Meg, this is not for the book."

I looked up at him, surprised. "But readers will be very interested to know about the stars over Algiers."

"You may write all you want about the stars, but not what I say next; it is my private thought."

"Your state of mind may stir your reader's sympathy. Trust me, Edward, to know what shall and shall not be put in a book of this sort."

He smiled. "I will trust you, then. But you must not be offended by what I say. Remember that I was grieving and heartsick, far from home."

"I will remember," I said, but I set my quill down upon the table after all.

"There was one night when I gazed upon the stars and yearned for a ship that would take me back to London. I had not let myself taste that longing for many weeks. And I thought to myself, Meg has sent me for a narrative of captivity, that is my Golden Fleece, which she asked me for only because she knew it was impossible. And if I can bring it back to her in spite of these terrible odds, she will love me after all, and things will end happily."

"Things did not end happily for Jason! He came back to find all his family murdered. You have had better luck."

For a moment he said nothing, and in the silence I saw that once again I had been cruel without intention. I felt how much a man like Edward deserved a thoughtful answer when he spoke of love, and I was in despair, for over and over I made the same mistakes. It was for such reasons as this that he had written in his volume, *I hate her*.

He must have felt something like, for at last, with incredulity in his voice, he said to me, "I don't know how Mr. Barlow manages to woo you. It seems everything is a romance to you except what concerns yourself."

"He does not bother, of course. Surely you know that love is wasted on me." I stood and gathered my pages together as quickly as I could. "I must go, I have been away from home many hours."

I looked toward the window, to judge the sun—and saw Will Barlow staring in at me.

As I spied him he turned, and went swiftly away. "Will!" I called, foolishly, for he was gone. "He saw us, through the window!" I said to Edward.

"I am sorry your secret is discovered," he said as he watched me. "But what did he see, that you need be ashamed? We are not lovers, after all."

Perhaps he meant to reassure me, but all I felt was woe. Indeed, I *was* ashamed, of all the lies that I had told, and of the long way I had come since the day I would not go into the Three Bells with Anne because it was a Sunday.

ᨳ 4 ᨳ

It was Deb who let me into the house. "You are to go to your father in the parlor," she said with an anxious look, so I knew the storm had already begun.

"Where is my stepmother?" I asked, for Susannah was sometimes able to calm my father when he grew angry, and though I did not think she would take my part, I hoped she would help my father to moderate his rage for his own sake. But Deb said she had gone to pay a visit, so I smoothed down my skirt and went to greet my father.

"Sit down, Daughter," he said the moment I entered the room.

I did so, and he sat opposite me, and looked at my face a long moment, as though he could read in it all he wished to know.

"Will Barlow says that he saw you alone with a man in a tavern," he said. "But I told him it could not be true. It is not true, is it, Margaret?"

"It is true. But I was not—"

"It is true." My father pressed his hands to the sides of his head and closed his eyes, as though he had heard something he could not bear.

"There has been no wrongdoing, Father."

"No wrongdoing! Will says you have been with this man many times, that you have been lying to us and sneaking off to meet him, is that also true?"

"Why do you say, 'this man'—did Will not tell you it is Edward Gosse I meet with?"

"Do you think it matters to me if it was Edward Gosse or the Bishop of Rome who has had his hand up your skirt!"

I jumped to my feet. "He has not! He has not! Did Will Barlow say that he saw such a thing?"

"Sit down!" my father thundered, and I did. "I am not a fool, Daughter. Because Will did not see you at a guilty moment does not mean there was no such moment. Why does a maid meet secretly with a man, after all? If he meant to court you, he would have come to me. You don't try to tell me that he means to court you?"

I paused before I replied. To my father all was yea or nay, but I could have given a dozen answers, and some of those were just unfolding themselves to me, like late-blooming flowers. "We meet that I might write a narrative of his captivity in Algiers," I said at last.

I could see in his face that he believed me at once—he believed me and was enraged. Now it was he that jumped to his feet, and walked about the parlor as he shouted at me. "Did I not forbid you such activity? And instead of obedience, you practice defiance. You gad about endangering your reputation, creating scandal, exposing yourself to ridicule. You are a willful, disobedient, cunning, deceitful maid, who does not deserve the protection of her father! What demon possesses you, Daughter, that has made you cast aside every loving-kindness you have received from your father and your stepmother? I have stood by you, even after I married again and begat heirs, I have offered you a handsome dowry, I have looked to your happiness in marriage, I have let you neglect your household duties that you might moon over your storybooks, by God, what have I not done for you! And you would not do this one small thing for me. You bewilder me, Daughter. I cannot conceive of your ingratitude."

I sat in silence as tears pricked my eyes. I did not try to answer him—what answer was there to such a just rebuke? There was none, except to offer my penitent apologies, and to swear I would never write again, and to tear up all my works and notes before my father's face. But I knew I would not do that.

As he ranted I began to be afraid of what would follow from his anger. A beating I could endure, but what if he were to cast me out, without support or protection? Would Edward let me serve at the Three Bells? But there I would indeed be at the mercy of every lascivious man with a cup of wine in his hand. Unless Edward offered me his protection? Would he be so kind to someone who had been cruel to him?

"You are like a dog born without a tail, or a goat with two heads, you are not natural!" my father said. "Would that you had married at fourteen, and were your husband's problem!"

Or perhaps my father would marry me off at once, to Will, and I would be exiled to Bristol, and never see London again, but would write in secret and burn my words in the grate, as Edward had foretold. Though my father could not force me to marry, he could withhold my dowry, and without it, who would have me? The crier who sold yardsticks in the street, perhaps, or the one who sold ink and quills, yes, that would be better, and I could demonstrate the fineness of our products, or write letters for illiterate seamen for a penny and so contribute to the family coffers.

"... to mitigate my wrath?"

I blinked. I had not expected a question, and so had not attended.

"What do you have to say on your own behalf, Child?"

He had come to the point where he wanted me to argue for myself. He always did come there, sooner or later, and I would have done better to spend my time arranging my thoughts than imagining unlikely futures for myself. But that was what I always did: imagine.

"I wish I had not lied," I said. "I wish there had been another way."

"There was the way of obedience."

"You call it a little thing, but to me it is not little. It is as if my stepmother said to you: Won't you give up reading, it is such a little thing."

"That is nonsense." He came back to his chair and sat once more. "Reading is part of my work."

"You have made it part of your work, because you love it."

"And have I ever forbidden you to read? You read every infamous thing that comes into the shop!"

"If it is so terrible a thing for a woman to write, why do we sell the works of Mademoiselle de Scudéry and Mademoiselle de la Roche-Guilhen? Why do you go to see the plays that were written by Aphra Behn? Why do you have a volume of Katherine Philips's verses in your chamber?"

"I will throw it into the fire tonight if you will swear to give up this foolishness."

"That is no answer."

"Meg, do you not know what is said of those women? Every scandalous accusation possible is made against Mrs. Behn! And Mrs. Philips lived in London while her husband lived in Wales! As for the others—they are French."

"I don't care what is said of me."

"That is true of no one. It is only true that for some, the pain of censure is not so great as the pain of deprivation."

I considered this. "I would rather have the pain of censure than to give over this work before it is complete."

"Oh, Meg! What am I to do with you?"

"Then I may finish?"

"Of course you may not finish! I will not reward your lying and disobedience with my approval! As a man of good conscience, how could I do such a thing?"

I looked into my lap at my folded hands. I had come so quickly into the room that I had not yet taken off my gloves. "I don't know, sir," I said in a low voice. I felt the sting of shame, remembering how lightly I had withheld the truth from him. I thought that of all my imaginings, this had been the wildest: that words upon a page could shed so bright a light that it would blind my father to the fact that I had deceived him.

"You must promise that you will not continue with this mad project. Do I have your word, Margaret?"

How could I fail to give it? And yet I did not bring forth the obedient answer that hovered on my tongue. I paused a moment to compose my voice, so that there would be nothing strident in it, and nothing of cajolery. I willed it to carry only the honor and esteem in which I held my father. "You have said that any words I write must not come to the ears of others," I began. "But would it be so bad, if they were to come to *your* ears, your ears only? Do you think it wrong, sir, for a parent to read the words his child has written?"

He leaned back in his chair and regarded me carefully, as though he suspected me of trickery. "You would not gain much by my reading it," he said.

"It would give me peace of mind. If you were to read my narrative, read it as though it had been written by Edward himself, or some other of your sex, and tell me if you think it worth printing—that would content me. I do not ask you to print it, only to tell me if you would do so if it had come from another pen."

"How many pages is the narrative?"

"Why—it has not been written yet, except the start, though I have made many notes, and have sketched a plan of the whole. I have waited to do most of the work because I meant to interview Mr. Gosse once more." As I said this I thought for the first time of what it would mean to Edward to stop now, and I felt my throat grow tight.

"Then you wish to show me only the start of your narrative?"

It was not what I wished. I sighed, and began to tug at my gloves. As I pulled off the right glove I saw a large ink stain upon my thumb. My father's eyes, too, fell upon it, and he looked at it for a long moment. Then he seemed to think that I had spoken, for he shook his head, and said, "You may not go with a man to a tavern. How can you think that I would countenance such a meeting?"

I looked up quickly. "We need not meet at the Three Bells. We might meet at Anne's, or at the Gosse house in Broad Street."

"I would have to interview Mr. Gosse," he said. "I would need his surety of good behavior, as well as yours, before you could meet again."

"I am sure he could satisfy you."

"He may. He may not. We will see."

I did not dare to fly at him with an embrace; I did not dare even to smile, but sat with my fingers laced while he called Deb to fetch Will to the parlor.

Ordinarily Will would not have been home, on a Sunday evening. He would have been abroad, perhaps watching the cocks fight, or drinking sack at a tavern. But today he had chosen otherwise.

"Sir?" he said to my father when he entered the room.

"Meg, say to Will what you have said to me, about the nature of your business with Edward Gosse."

"We met so that I might write a narrative of his captivity. That is all. How could you think otherwise, Mr. Barlow?"

He did not answer, but his face was proud and angry, and I could see that he had words he dared not say before my father.

"Do you doubt me?" I asked, dismayed.

"He does not doubt you," my father said with authority. "And nothing that passes his lips will subject your reputation to doubt or scandal, is that not right, Will?"

"Yes, sir," Will said obediently. He was dismissed, and left the house at once. We heard the front door slam.

I did not see Will again that day, for he was not at evening prayers. I saw him the next day, and the next, but we were never alone, and his speeches were brief and without warmth. When three days had passed, we were at last in the shop together, and only old Mr. Maynard was with us. He had come in for one of Dean Stillingfleet's sermons, and when we did not have it, he stayed long, looking at every bound and unbound book he thought that he might like to buy in its stead. But in the end I persuaded him to go away empty-handed.

As soon as he was gone I demanded of Will, "How could you think it of me?"

"What else was I to think? If your meetings were innocent, why were they also secret?"

"That I might avoid your dispraise. I have heard your remarks upon women authors."

"Must I change my views, because you don't share them?"

"Must I expose myself to your censure, because I write?"

"It is your bad judgment that I censure, madame."

The formality and unpleasantness of his words made a cold place within me, but I answered with heat. "Someday, when I am married, I will have a husband who does not start and tremble with fear that his wife's reputation will be tarnished by idle tongues!"

"He will not be a bookseller, then, for such a man must always concern himself with what is said in Town."

For a single second I wondered if there was still time for us to unsay our hasty words, and save our bookshop, that now foundered before the signboard was even hung. But in truth, I knew that it was over, and I could not regret it.

When I spoke it was not in anger, but in apology. "No," I said. "My husband will not be a bookseller."

His face filled with disdain, but I knew that in his heart it was otherwise, and I pitied him. However, he had his anger to console him, and his pride, and all the virtues of an Englishman, besides.

Ten

Though my father had told me he would send for Edward, he did not do so for several days. Perhaps he hoped that I would give up the narrative after all, or perhaps he only forgot—he had many things to think of besides a wayward daughter. The day after I spoke with Will, I could not bear the wait anymore, and I reminded my father of his words. The next afternoon he sent his apprentice from the shop, and summoned Edward there to see him.

I was waiting on Mr. Miller when Edward entered. I did not take my eyes from my customer, yet I knew who had come.

"But is there *another* history that would be better?" Mr. Miller asked me. "Does this one say why the fire traveled as it did, and just how it was stopped at last, and what the Papists meant by setting it?"

I had read the account of the Great Fire he held in his

hand and it did not tell any of those things, but I was anxious that he should leave at once. "It is the best history yet written of the disaster," I assured him, and took his shillings.

When Mr. Miller had left I stole a look at Edward as he greeted my father. He was more carefully dressed than usual; his suit was fine, and he wore a sword at his side. And yet his clothes did not become him. He did not look like a man of means and fashion, but like a man who is trying to be what he is not, and I felt vexed when I regarded him, and wished he had taken more care before he presented himself to my father.

He did not glance my way.

"Shall I go, sir?" I asked my father as the two of them settled into chairs before the fire.

"No, Meg, it is well that you should hear what I say to Mr. Gosse upon this subject," he replied. And then, to Edward, "Do you know why I have asked you to come?"

"If I am not mistaken, sir, your apprentice has misrepresented to you my meeting with your daughter."

"If Mr. Barlow misunderstood what he saw, that is hardly surprising," my father said. "Meg has told me what the two of you have been at, and I believe her, but I am sorry and displeased that you should have given way to her persuasion in this matter of your narrative. You ought to have been left alone after your ordeal."

"It was she who gave way to my persuasion. I wanted to tell my story, and knew her to be skilled with words."

"You cannot have known, surely, that she had been forbidden such activity?"

"I did not know it when I sought her help. She told me later, however."

"Yet you continued to meet?" my father asked with astonishment.

"Yes, sir. I did not like to make her choices for her."

"Then you encouraged her in her disobedience?"

"I do not value obedience so highly as I did before I was a slave, sir."

I wanted to bury my face in my hands. Why must Edward speak of such things now—did he not know how close we were to losing everything?

"That is a dangerous path," my father answered him, mildly enough. "We are all bound by something in this life. If we have no masters, we have yet duties to those who rank above us, and again to those who depend upon us. Is that not so?"

"It is so, sir."

"And yet, should all authority be turned upon its head, so that the thief does not regard the constable, or the Parliament regard the King?"

"But the thief does *not* regard the constable," I pointed out.

"Therefore he hangs. Be silent, Daughter, it is not with you that I debate."

"I do not speak of great matters such as these, Mr. Moore," Edward said. "I speak only of this small bond between my story and Meg's pen. I allow that it was eccentric—to place that bond above your authority. I do not believe it was wrong, sir."

I nearly gasped, and my father started, so that the curls of his wig began to bounce. I do not know which of us felt the greater shock. I have never been fired upon by pirates, nor been beaten upon the soles of my feet, so I do not know how much courage it may take to undergo those hardships. But I know that few men are brave enough to speak to my father the way Edward did that day.

"Certainly it was wrong, Mr. Gosse," my father said with vigor.

"Men of good character may differ on such a point. I have used my best judgment, Mr. Moore."

My father did not reply at once, but took up his pipe and began to fill it. I looked from the older to the younger man, wondering with dismay if Edward's rashness would after all prevent the completion of our narrative. He, too, awaited my father's next words. His face revealed nothing, except, perhaps, that he was not a happy man.

My father lit his pipe from a candle, and pulled the smoke in, and let it out into the shop, where its scent mixed with the smells of ink and beeswax. "I hope that you will learn greater wisdom as the years pass, Mr. Gosse. But let us speak now of this narrative. I have told Meg that it cannot be printed."

Edward's displeasure showed upon his face. "I am sorry to hear it, sir."

"It is your wish that your perils and sufferings be published to all the kingdom?"

"Not my perils and sufferings only, but all my experience of Algiers. If the entire story were told, then, yes, I would be content."

"It is strange to me that it is not enough for your contentment to find yourself in a Christian nation once more, prosperous and free."

"Would it not be well for those in London to learn something of these people, with whom we have more and more to do? There was a treaty signed in April, you know, between our kingdom and Algiers. Who knows what sort of future will follow?"

My father exhaled deeply, and the smoke drifted toward the door. "Your project may be a worthy one, Mr. Gosse, but that is not the point. If you had come to me, things would be different. But you did not."

"No, sir. I did not."

I do not know how he made his simple agreement sound so very pointed, but I was not the only one who took his meaning.

"You chose my daughter to write your story for you, and now you must bear the consequences of your choice. However, I have told her she may finish this narrative if she likes—that she may interview you once more, and write the thing, and I have promised to read it. Not with a view to printing it, you understand."

"I understand, sir."

"And you still wish to finish?"

"I do, sir."

"Of course, she cannot meet at a tavern with a man. She has suggested that the final interview can be finished at Mrs. Rushworth's lodgings, or at your mother's—as should have happened from the start. I assume you have no objection?"

"No, sir."

"You do not intend to court her?"

I felt myself go scarlet, and looked down at the ledger that was still open upon the counter. I had not expected my father to raise this subject.

"No, sir." Had there been the slightest of pauses before he answered? I was not sure.

My father coughed a little from the harshness of the tobacco. "If that should change, I trust you are not so eccentric that you would take it upon yourself to do so without her father's consent?"

"No, sir."

Finally I dared to raise my eyes, but I need not have bothered; Edward was not looking at me. I do not believe he had looked at me since entering the shop.

When he was gone my father puffed thoughtfully on his pipe. "A man who does not think as other men do will always be a danger to society," he said.

"How can you say so, Father? Think of all the poets with whom you are acquainted, or the men in the Royal Society, who look through microscopes at the tiniest things in creation, or through telescopes at the ones farthest away. Do they think like other men?"

"They do not," my father said. "And every one of them is dangerous."

━━ 2 ━━

It was at the Gosse house, on Broad Street, that Edward and I met one afternoon late in May. Anne was drawing very near the time of her confinement, and had gossips with her almost always; there was no room at Salisbury Court for business that had naught to do with babies.

Edward had prepared for us a small table in the best parlor, spread with writing tools, as our table at the tavern had always been, and situated near the window so the light was good. His mother was at the Three Bells, of course, but his sister, Gertrude, who was fourteen, sat in a chair in the corner with some mending.

"It is all very proper," I said as I sat down. "But I confess I miss our workroom at the Bells. I had only to close my eyes there, to see the sun shining on the bright tiles of Algerine buildings."

"It does not matter," Edward said. "Our work is almost done."

I could see from his face that he was not in good humor, which vexed me, for I had brought some scenes to show him, and I knew he would find fault with them. But

I could not delay. Now that my father knew of our project, we were hurried in a way we had not been before.

"I am sorry my father will not yield. Perhaps when it is finished you can take the narrative to another publisher and present it as your own work."

He looked at me for a brief moment. I think it was the first time our eyes had met since he had said, *We are not lovers.* But I could not read his thought.

"We need not think of that yet," he said.

I reached into my bag. "It is time for you to read some of what I have written," I said, and offered him a sheaf of pages.

He took them without reply and began to read.

Do all writers know their pages as I know mine? Every flaw and crease and blot upon the paper was familiar to me, so that when I saw Edward's thumb near the *s* where I had splattered ink, I knew he read of the shining sun, and when his eyes traveled below the fold, I knew he read of the boy.

He stopped, there, and said to me gravely, "You have spared me."

"I have told the truth," I said.

He shook his head, and read aloud from the page, " 'The boy cried out for my aid, and I was much distressed because I could not help him.' "

"Did he not call out for your aid?"

"I have told you so."

"Were you not in great distress, because you had none to give?"

"I was distressed. But who can be certain I had no help to give? If I had been bolder . . ."

"We need not worry about degrees of certainty, as if we were philosophers. It is enough for us to use our common understanding, which tells us that if you had turned and fought, Christopher Hughes would have been sold in the marketplace just the same."

"Perhaps."

"And it is likely that you yourself would have died that day, and left so many of us here in London sore with grief. Thank God you did not do it, Edward."

He looked up again, and for a moment he did not speak. Then he said, "It was not easy for me to tell the truth about what passed in Algiers. For what cause did I work so hard, if I am only to be spared at last?"

I had myself thought much on that, and knew my answer. "In art, every hard truth must be put in at first, it is what fuels the fire. But when the blaze is burning, much must be fished out again with tongs. Consider this. You wish to reveal to your readers a city called Algiers, about which you have learned some things that few Western men know. If you would be believed, you must first earn the trust of your audience, and persuade them that you are a man of character and Christian virtue. You dare not flay yourself before them, Edward, as you have done before me." I saw from his face that it had given him pain to hear me, and added, "Remember that they do not know your worth as I do; they do not know, as I do, how unjust you have been to yourself."

"In what manner unjust? I do not see that I have been unjust."

"Of course you have been unjust. Everything of which you accuse yourself comes in the end to one fact: You were a slave, which should not have been, and you blame yourself because you could not prevent it or unmake it. I do not know if the stamp of that can ever leave a man. But I know 'twas not your fault—as you know it was not mine."

He looked at me long, and I wondered if his gray eyes were blue when he was by the Mediterranean. "I think you are overgentle with me," he said at last. "But I will not mind if others blame me, while you do not."

And I knew he did not hate me, after all.

He lowered his eyes once more to my work, but I no longer marked where upon the page he read. I wanted to jump to my feet, and pace the room as he had done so often at the Three Bells, because he did not hate me. But instead I laced my fingers tightly together and waited with poor patience for him to finish.

After a little he said, "You have got Christopher's age wrong. He was twelve, not ten."

"I did not get it wrong. I altered it, that our readers might have more sympathy for him."

"You have no regard for the truth."

"What have I told our readers that is not true? From this they know that a boy was orphaned, who should not have been. I do not want them saying to themselves, 'After all, at twelve a boy is old enough to take the Oath of Allegiance.'"

Again he read. I watched the pages pass, marking when he read of the moment he left the hold of the ship, and walked once more beneath the dazzling sun; and when he read of the children who gathered around him, staring at his yellow hair; and when of the first time he spoke in Arabic, and startled those who marched him along the shore.

At last he said, "There was no such contest as you describe, to bid for me. There was no rivalry between a kind Arab and a cruel one, to take me home."

"It will attach the reader to your cause, however, and lead him to read on with great interest, so that by the time you speak of mosques and minarets, he will be attending to every word you have written."

"To every word *you* have written."

"It does not matter, does it, who has written them, as long as they have been true? I do not mean true in every detail—how can that matter? But true in their essence, in their root, if you like. If our narrative is true, it will shine a light upon the place you were, and the people you met there. If it does not do that, tell me, please, and we will put these pages in the fire, and begin again."

I waited without breath for his reply, which was long in coming. I glanced at his sister, and saw that she was waiting, too. At last he said, "We need not do that. The light shines."

Then I breathed again, and Gertrude bent over her work, and the servant came into the room with some biscuits and ale. The relief I felt taught me that I wanted nothing more in life, ever, than to make the light shine, even if it must do so under a bushel basket, even if I must give up bookselling and marriage both, and must live in dire poverty, and write by candlelight while others slept until my sight was ruined, and die at last at an early age, leaving naught but verses to my heirs. Indeed, I was so eager to make sacrifices that I could not think of enough, now that I had heard Edward say: *The light shines.*

When he had read all I gave him, Edward said, "It is not done."

"Of course it is not. That is why I have come." I pulled a fresh page to me, and picked up a quill. "You spoke of your new master, who showed you the stars over Algiers."

"Yes, of Omar. This is the part of the story that took the longer to live, and changed my heart the most, and yet it is shortest in the telling."

"It is often that way."

"More and more, Omar and I passed the hours together. He had no son, have I told you? And his daughter married in the autumn."

My hand paused in its work. "He had a daughter?"

"Yes. I was at her wedding feast. I have told you of that. Omar treated me with great kindness, as though I were indeed his son—my own father was not a kinder man. We talked for hours, and my Arabic grew faster and fuller. The throat must open and close to pronounce the gutturals of that language, you know, and at first it is not easy for a Western man. But in time my throat did what it must without my command, for I had become as accustomed to Arabic as to *couscous*, or the brightness of the light. Omar told me much about the history of Algiers, but he liked most to speak of the history of Islam. He was a man of great devotion. There were many such in Algiers; the name of God was always on their breath. My master had memorized much of the Qur'an, or perhaps he knew it all, I could not tell. Every day he would recite a part of it aloud, and the next day a different part, so that when some weeks had passed, he had said it all, I believe, and began again. Imagine if the word of God were so graven on Christian hearts!"

"But the Qur'an is not the word of God," I reminded him.

He did not answer, which made me uneasy. I thought how I might lead him to a different subject, but before I could speak he burst out, "I wish that I could show you Algiers, Meg! I wish that you could view it from the sea—it is beautiful! It is set upon a hill, and the roofs of the houses are whitened with lime, so that the city shines in the sun. There is a breakwater built of stone that stretches across the bay, and the sea itself is such a color there—I do not think that color exists in England. Great castles guard the city, and the domes of the mosques gleam like gold. Once I spoke of its beauty to Omar, and he said, 'In the spring I shall take you to Cairo; that is a city worth seeing.' And he told me of the pyramids, and the river Nile that is so famous, and the narrow streets of the city, and the great and stately mosques. There are minarets there circled by two or three balconies, he said, and at Ramadan they are illuminated with many lamps, and are glorious to behold. I listened to all he said, and asked many questions, and learned much. There are Christians there that are called Coptics, who wear turbans even as Muslims do. And Omar said that there are *seventy-two* languages spoken in Cairo. Seventy-two, Meg!"

And he looked to me for my response. All this time I had written busily, but so many feelings warred in me I hardly could distinguish them. I saw the Moorish cities as he painted them, and almost envied him because he had seen them and I had not, which was foolish, for I would not have wished to pay the price he paid. At the same time I did not like how he spoke of these places, as though they rivaled London. When he paused I could not keep from saying, "I do not see how you can so love a place that was your prison."

He nodded thoughtfully, and put a hand to his beard as though the touch of it helped him to think. Then he said, "When a man has suffered greatly, and then is rescued from that suffering, and treated with love, he is changed. And time—time does much, and I was there many months. I learned to love *couscous*, which I will never taste again, and the lamb cooked with nuts and fruits the family ate when they broke their fast after darkness fell, in the season of Ramadan. Was I to hate the mild evenings, when I sat with my master in the courtyard of his home and ate dates from a bowl? Here I would have been huddled before a fire. Was I to hate the castles and the mosques, that were so beautiful? The pillars, the courtyards? The figs that cost so much here in England? Or the Turkish coffee? I did not hate these things. I did not hate living among turbaned people. I did not hate the chant of the *muezzin* who calls the Muslims to prayer from the top of a minaret five times in a day."

"So many!"

"Indeed." Suddenly he threw back his head and called loudly in a foreign tongue, in open sounds that lingered and hummed, and other sounds that were so sharp and sudden they cut like knives across his syllables. His voice on the air was so alien that I started, and Gertrude in her corner gasped. I looked anxiously at the door, as though I feared a justice were on the other side, for it seemed not safe nor lawful for him to speak in that language. But Edward did not mark us. I looked at his mouth thrown open and the beard that trailed from his chin, and thought that there was something, not only in his words, but in his manner, that was unfettered and otherlandish, and had never been learned in London.

When he was done, it was as if something of Algiers had been left behind in the room: some white light or warm wind or scent of desert fruit. He did not translate, but said, "They pray with their bodies, Meg, as well as their voices. They sit upon their legs and touch their foreheads to the ground. And always they face Mecca as they pray; it is their holy city. My master had a globe that showed the stars, and with it he could make many calculations. He could calculate the direction of Mecca from different cities."

"That is interesting," I admitted, beginning to write once more.

"I asked him, once, to make that calculation for London."

"Edward, no!"

"I was only curious. Of course, a Muslim could not live freely in England as a Christian may in Algiers."

"Surely they are great persecutors of Christians."

"No, Christians gathered together to worship in Algiers, and were not interfered with. Only, if a man should convert to Islam, then he must keep that faith all his life. If he should change his heart a second time, they will kill him."

"That is terrible!"

Edward shrugged. "It is all done according to law. There is much killing in the world over differences of faith. How many Papists were executed last year?"

"They had a plot to kill the King," I pointed out.

"Who believes that, now?" he said, and I made no answer, because most men of good sense no longer believed there had ever been such a plot, and some said that the King's enemies had only been using the fears of the people to make themselves stronger in Parliament. "Did your master try to convert you to his religion?" I asked.

Edward hesitated. "He spoke of his faith often," he said. "I think he would have been happy if I had embraced Islam. But he never suggested it himself. The Muslims are wary of men who claim to love the Prophet Muhammad only so that they may gain their freedom. But certainly many Christians have feigned conversion for that end."

"You yourself did not think of turning renegade!" I said, thinking of his strange call.

"No," he said slowly, "It was not like that. I rather longed to love my own faith the way I saw my master loving his. Listening to him recite the Qur'an gave me a kind of yearning that I do not think can ever be satisfied."

"You must not say so, Edward."

He smiled a little. "There are so many things I must not say. Perhaps you will find a way to say them that the world can bear to hear."

I cast sand upon my finished page, and drew a new one to me. "What more, Edward?" I asked.

He considered a little and then offered me his open palms. "It seems we are finished at last," he said.

"Nay, you have not yet told me of the moment you heard that you were ransomed. Your readers will want to hear of that, for it is a kind of pinnacle to our story."

I said this unhappily, for I could see already that he would tell me things that brought me grief. But I did not try, this time, to put words into his mouth. I did not say, *And you rejoiced to learn that you were free.* For I knew that it was not so.

He glanced at me, and seemed to know my thoughts. "I think we must leave our pinnacle unscaled, Meg."

But of course that was not possible. "You cannot flinch now, at the end."

He drew in breath, and began again. "When I first waited to be ransomed, I wanted nothing but my home, nothing! I wanted to return to London as quickly as possible, I wanted everything to be as it once was. I only endured the hours by thinking of the narrative we would write when I returned one day. Every drop of sweat, every mouthful of food, every stinking camel, every bright tile, every Arab robe that flapped in the wind—I stored these things up to tell you. When I had been passed to a second master, the things I gathered for you had greater import, for Omar and I discussed matters of history, of language and religion. 'Ah,' I would say to myself, 'Meg will be so interested to learn of this.'

"For a long, long time, my thoughts of you—my thoughts of home, that is to say—were more real than any life I knew in North Africa. But time passed, and at last I truly lived in Algiers, and not in London at all. And I did not save up things to tell you anymore."

I could not bear to hear any further explanations, for I knew he only delayed the saying of painful words. "And when you first heard that you were ransomed?" I pressed him.

He paused only a moment, and then said what I had waited to hear. "At first I thought only, 'Now I must go back. Now I lose my father a second time. Now I will never see Cairo.' "

It was not how I had imagined it, when I had gained the last shilling needed to bring him home. I laid my pen upon the table, hoping that he would stop, for I did not want to hear another word from him. But he did not stop.

"It is not that I was ungrateful, Meg. I have said little of my thankfulness to you only because I feel how small a thing gratitude is against the largeness of what you have done for me. Even if slavery comes to be—I will not say welcome, but in some way soft, perhaps—there is always the shame of knowing that you do not do your duty in the world, but only help another to do his. You cannot be a slave and still feel that you are a man.

"But by the time I was indeed ransomed—by then I knew that nothing could be as it had been before. The day I left this Town I belonged here as a foot belongs in a well-worn boot. But, Meg—look at me, Meg." But I would not. "London does not *fit* me now, it rubs me until I am blistered. Perhaps it is the stamp of slavery that you speak of, or perhaps it is only that foreign winds have blown through me and left me changed. But I am no longer like other men. I pass the time with them in the tavern or the coffee-house, but I am always straining to find the thing I ought to say. I only pretend, now, to be an Englishman."

I thought to tell him that all Englishmen were not the same, that Mr. Winter did not see eye to eye with my father, nor the Duke of York with Lord Shaftesbury; that there were Englishmen who made their home in Virginia now, and in the Indies, who must also be different than they had been before.

But other words found their way to my tongue. "I know something of what that is like. All my life I have felt—different. Different from my father's wife, or from your sister, Anne. My father says that I am unnatural, like a goat with two heads."

He made a quick movement, and started to speak, but stopped himself. At last he said, "A man of your father's age does not change his ideas easily. Mr. Barlow will be different, I am sure."

"Mr. Barlow's views on the matter are no longer of consequence." I did not look at him as I spoke.

He was very still for a moment. Then he said, "I will not lie and say that I am sorry. But if your heart is sore—I am sorry for that."

"It was never a matter of my heart, Edward. Have I not told you that I am practical? Only I think that matrimony is *not* very practical for a woman who believes herself an author. How can such a woman work, when her humors are altered from breeding, or when children hang from her skirt, or when she must serve in her husband's business all day because times are hard or trade is brisk, or be watchful of her husband's moods, because his trials in life have made him choleric or sullen?"

"You speak of me," he said. "You speak of me!" He was greatly agitated. He got to his feet, and turned to look at his sister, who scuttled from the room as though he had given her a command.

I was embarrassed, for I had not meant to voice my thought so clearly. But before I could beg pardon, he turned to me, and spoke calmly, as one who debates. "Let us be fair," he said. "There are risks on both sides. If we were to wed, think what would be my part! I would have to eat your burnt biscuits, and hear your ill-timed jests, and bear the scorn of men who believe that a woman who is an author cannot also be virtuous."

Now I felt a blush travel from my cheeks until all my face was warm. "Then it is surely wiser not to venture," I said.

"Perhaps. Perhaps. We cannot see our futures. It might be, if we were to marry, that you would die within a year, in childbed, or I would be taken off by a chill after five, and leave you alone with little ones to rear. Or it might fall out differently." He took his seat again, opposite me, and regarded me intently. "Perhaps we would put Henry to mind the warehouse, and sail to the Mediterranean, to trade in sherry and Madeira. We might live in Livorno, and teach our children to speak Italian, and visit Cairo at Ramadan, or perhaps I would take you to see the white roofs of Algiers."

He paused, but I could not speak. It was clear that Edward had thought many times of such a future, but to me it was new, and my breath caught as the vision unfolded before me.

"It is only fair to imagine the good as well as the bad, after all," he said gently, "though I allow it is less likely to happen. More often, those we love die in our arms, and our fortunes founder, and our dearest projects are left incomplete, because our powers fail us. Yes, these things are very common, are they not? It is just for this reason that it is hard to go through life alone. But if you have courage enough—why, then, I admire you, Meg."

My heart was very full, and I knew not what answer to make. But he did not wait for one.

"I am foolish to speak to you in this way!" he exclaimed suddenly. "I will waste no more time."

I looked up quickly when he said that, with a protest on my lips—then saw that he was smiling. "I will not be eccentric," he said. "I have promised to go first to your father. Then I will have more to say on this subject. It may be that I do not succeed—with him, or with you. But I will chance my luck."

⤝ 3 ⤜

The next day, with my father's leave, I did not go to the shop, but spread my papers on the hinged table in the parlor. It was strange indeed to look over my many pages of shorthand, and to see upon them Edward's journey completed: his fears and shames revealed, his observations noted, his reason asserted, his hopes altered. Most of these notes I had read many times. I had shuffled the sentences as though they were cards, I had sorted his thoughts, shaped his adventures, watched his words change into mine. And yet the thing was not done, and still I pondered how I might make from such material a narrative that would both honor the teller and satisfy the needs of the told; how I might relate enough of truth that our readers would scent it, and draw near, as a doe to water, but not so

much that it would frighten them away with the sound of
its splashing.

I took a fresh page and wrote upon it:

Courteous Reader,
Perhaps no sort of writing is as liable to abuse as that
of the narrative. Tales of every kind beckon the credu-
lous reader: stories of the soldier who is crowned with
glory as he dies upon the battlefield, or of the heroic
apprentice who overcomes an evil duke to win fair
maiden; stories that show, in all their bright splendor,
the marvelous beasts that travelers have seen in far-off
lands.

And every author vows that his tale is true in each
particular. Every dying speech is vouched for; every
gryphon, roc, and phoenix is sworn to be authentic. It
is no wonder, then, if a reader grows wary of these
narratives, in which he finds upon the page marvels
and miracles that he never himself beheld.

If you are in search of such diversions, dear
Reader, you must look elsewhere, for herein lie only the
simplest of verities, the plainest of truths. It is not for
me to say whether anyone may benefit from such
points of information as will be found in the pages
that follow. But be ye assured that all such facts are
genuine and authentic, to the best of this traveler's ob-
servation.

I have held myself to a hard law in reporting to

you all that I have heard and seen and learned in the city of Algiers, in the land which some call Barbary. But the mind of man is not like the secretary who keeps the minutes of a meeting. It is like a mixing bowl, into which all things fall, but when those things are taken out again, the nutmeg can no longer be separated from the salt, nor the milk from the egg. Though everything I have written in this narrative is true, no truth is untouched by what I learned in Algiers.

Lastly, Courteous Reader, though I do not offer you gryphons or centaurs, it is well to know that among these pages you will indeed journey in a place that is like unto a story land. Do not for that reason doubt what you read. Many places exist that we have never seen with our own eyes. I have never seen the gold of the Andes, the pyramids of Egypt, or the kingdom of Heaven, but I do believe that they are real and true. And I tell you that the city of Algiers, the stars that shine above her, and all that befell me there of ill and of good, that, too, is real and true.

I am, Reader, thy friend and servant, Edward Gosse, Merchant.

As I read over what I had written, Deb came into the parlor. "A message has come, from Mrs. Gosse," she said. "She thought you would want to know that Mrs. Rushworth has begun her labor."

~~ 4 ~~

A nne's labor was long, but not longer than was safe, and at the proper time she gave birth to a well-formed boy. I was relieved at the ease of her delivery, but not surprised, for Mrs. Gosse had borne many children and had lost only two. But at the same time I envied her, because I knew that she had now begun the work she most longed to do. If fortune was kind, she would watch her son grow, she would teach him his manners, and his letters, and such essential virtues as charity, forbearance, and prudence. When the time was right he would leave off coats and put on breeches, and at length he would go to school, and later would be apprenticed, and someday he would marry and take his place in the world. And all that time Anne would watch him, and beam when he was praised, and suffer on his behalf when he was affronted.

I wanted to see my work, too, go out into the world.

It was on an evening late in June that I brought the narrative at last to my father, and told him it was ready for his judgment. He took it as a man will take a coin that he doubts, before he tests it between his teeth. I had many things ripe to tell him as I handed him the manuscript: explanations as to why I had done things one way instead of another, and apologies that it was not better. But most of all I had arguments to persuade him to publish it, for when the last *t* was crossed I believed it was a glorious and brave and true and faithful account of Edward's adventure, and I thought everyone in London would want to read it—and should.

But he was my father, so I said none of these ripe things, but instead took Toby to our chamber, and held him there upon my knee while I told him of St. George and the dragon, until he was drowsy, and tumbled into bed.

For three days I was nervous and cross, the way I am before my months. Susannah did not notice, but Will asked me what was wrong, which surprised me, for he rarely spoke to me now except to request my help in the most formal way he could.

"I have finished Mr. Gosse's narrative," I said to him. "My father reads it now, and I am anxious to know his mind."

"He is bound to admire it," Will said. "He is proud of everything you do."

I stared at him, but he had turned back to his ledgers, so I shook my head and returned to my book. I did not think my father was bound to admire my work, and if he did, I hoped it would not be because I was his daughter.

That night, as the household members scattered after evening prayers, my father summoned me. I stood before him, with my hands wrapped in my apron, and waited for his words. But for once they did not come readily to him, and he had to start and start again before at last he lifted my manuscript from the table and said, "It is fine, Margaret. I tell you nothing you do not know."

I had told myself I would not weep if he disliked it, but I had laid no such rule upon myself if it proved otherwise, so I permitted two hot tears to creep down my cheeks. "And you would print it, if it were not mine?" I asked him.

"I will print it, though it is."

It was what I had hoped to hear, yet I hardly believed him. I said nothing, but stopped my mouth with my hand, as though to keep my joy a secret.

"You need not thank me," he said, and I could not tell if he was more vexed with himself or more amused. "I do not do it for your sake; it is only that I am a better book-seller than a father. Of course, there will be changes—I must go over it with a pencil. But 'twill serve."

"I am so glad, Father!" I said finally.

"You need not think your name will be upon it."

"I do not care one whit!"

"That will not last," my father said gloomily. "Authors must have their notoriety. They cannot live without it." Then he stooped and kissed my brow. "It is very well done, Child."

I knew *that* was said for my sake, and it seemed to me the right moment to speak of another matter. "Its worth did not come from me alone, sir. It is Mr. Gosse's voice."

"His story, but your voice, I think."

"Perhaps. Mr. Gosse has been through many trials."

"Yes, I have read of them," my father said, tapping my pages.

"I think he has shown himself to be a man of good character, Father."

He scowled. "A man of good character will not encourage a maid in disobedience."

"Yet think what he has done since he returned to London. All the Town talks of how he has put the business right. He is a careful man, not profligate, and he takes his duty to his family very seriously. He has always been a good brother to Anne."

My father looked at me keenly. "In short, he is a man who will pay me a visit soon, to ask if I would look favorably upon his attempts to win my daughter."

"Yes, sir. He is."

"I will tell him that he is mad to want a wife who spends her time like this," he said, waving the narrative in the air. Then he bade me go to bed, and settled at the hinged table with my manuscript before him, and a pencil in his hand.

I was not present when Edward met with my father to discuss my future, but that did not keep me from guessing at what they said as I oiled the furniture in the parlor. I knew, of course, that they spoke of money, of Edward's obligations to his family, of our youth, and of the Court of Aldermen who must approve Edward's match. Did they also discuss my disobedience and Edward's wild views? Was Livorno mentioned? Did they speak of the narrative through which he and I had come to know and honor one another? I slid my rag across the hinged table where my father had studied my manuscript so lately. *A place that is like unto a story land*, I had written. Would I one day stand upon the deck of a ship with Edward beside me, and watch the glint of sun on quicklime as the rooftops of Algiers drew near? I found that I had ceased rubbing, and stood gazing at nothing. I laughed at myself, and moved to the walnut armchair, where I drew my rag over the scrollwork until it glistened. It would be marvelous indeed to see the blue of the Mediterranean someday, but if I did, it would be for a second time, as Edward had already taken me once upon that journey.

It rained all morning on St. Swithin's Day, but to me it mattered not. "I do not care if it rains till nightfall!" I said recklessly as I stood near the shop window, watching the downpour. They say if it rains on St. Swithin's Day, the next forty days will be wet as well, and the summer harvest will be spoiled.

"I care," Will said. "We are only half done with July, and I would like a few more summer days before the autumn rains begin. He will not come any faster, you know, because you push against the glass. Look, your breath has clouded it."

I came away from the window and walked to the fire, where I shook my skirt to let the warm air come within. Almost at once the door opened, and Edward entered.

"Has it come?" he asked as he removed his dripping hat.

"We wait for it now," I said.

"Anne sends her love, and would have come, except our mother insists she is not ready to leave her bed. But look, Meg, I have brought you something." He reached beneath his damp coat. "It is from France."

"Why, I have heard of these! Mr. Barker, the astrologer, has one. It is a pen that holds its own ink, is it not?"

"It is."

"What a curious thing. How sweet you are, to think of me!"

I longed to give him a kiss, as I would have done if we had been alone, but of course with Will there I could not, so instead I took his coat, and urged him to stand before the fire, and asked him if he had heard the rumor that Mr. Dryden's new play would be banned by the King.

At last the door opened again, and my father came within. At first it seemed he had no parcel, but of course he had put it beneath his coat, to save it from the weather. Now he took it out and placed it on the counter. We all looked at it a moment, as though we thought it would jump up and dance, and then Will reached out and tore the wrapping paper from the bundle, and we each of us took up a copy to peruse.

As I had promised my father, my name was not upon it anywhere, and as he had foretold, I felt a little pang at that, and hoped it would be different another time.

The door opened again, and Mr. Winter came in.

"I did not expect to see you on such a day, Mr. Winter!" my father exclaimed.

"I could not wait," Mr. Winter said, smiling. "I have brought my shilling. Is it here?"

And thus he kept his promise, and bought the first copy of the little stitched book which I had written, and which bore upon its cover these words:

Edward Gosse

A True and Faithful Narrative of his Capture & Enslavement by Barbary Pirates

Printed for Miles Moore
and sold at the sign of the Star

Author's Note: On Piracy

There is a long history in the Mediterranean of piracy and slavery. Though the Barbary corsairs are only one part of this history, they played a major role in world affairs for several centuries. The North African lands of Algiers, Tunisia, Tripoli, and Morocco captured citizens from many European countries and held them for ransom. Treaties were made between various nations and the different Barbary states from time to time, and sometimes an agreement was made to pay tribute in order to ensure safe passage of a country's vessels. But none of these agreements put an end to the practice of piracy.

In the late eighteenth and early nineteenth centuries, the new nation of the United States of America, whose citizens were also captured and enslaved, became a strong military force in the region and was instrumental in weakening the Barbary powers. When the Napoleonic Wars ended in 1815, European nations such as France and Italy joined the United States in its military assault on North Africa, and soon the former Barbary states became European colonies. Barbary piracy was at last at an end, though colonialism would bring its own injustices.

A number of captives who were ransomed or who escaped wrote about their experiences when they came home. Two of the accounts by Britons were especially helpful to me in writing *A True and Faithful Narrative*. One was written by Joseph Pitts, who was only fifteen years old when he was taken captive in 1678. He lived in Algiers and in Mecca until 1694, and during that time he converted to Islam and became a free man. Though his narrative includes an account of being taken captive, like Edward he is really more interested in talking about the customs of the Muslim peoples of North Africa.

The other story that interested me was that of William Okeley, who was a slave in Algiers from 1639 until his escape in 1644. Okeley didn't write his narrative himself, but, like Edward, told it to someone else, who wrote it down for him. We don't know this writer's name, but we know that he or she had a great storytelling gift and turned Okeley's experiences into a dramatic and compelling tale.

In order to communicate the flavor of seventeenth-century prose I committed a few small piracies of my own. The sermon at Philip Gosse's funeral, for example, uses language from two different preachers of the era. I borrowed the phrase "but his stars cast their malicious influence over the sea," which Meg uses in "Temptation in Algiers," from one of Aphra Behn's prose works. Meg's reflection "that bread was still dough, and who could say if it would ever rise?" was inspired by a similar metaphor used by Samuel Pepys in his diary, and her accusation that Muhammad was a cobbler is from Okeley's account of his captivity in Algiers. Edward's story about enraging his first master with criticisms of Islam is also closely based on an incident in Okeley's narrative. Finally, when Meg writes her introduction to Edward's story, she echoes other captivity memoirs when she writes "I have held myself to a hard law," and "It is not for me to say whether anyone may benefit from such points of information as will be found in the pages that follow." In fact, Meg borrows closely from Okeley's work with her very first sentence: "Perhaps no sort of writing is as liable to abuse as that of the narrative."

In order to write *A True and Faithful Narrative* I became intensely absorbed in Meg's world, which was wonderful for me but not always easy for those around me. No amount of gratitude can ever repay my husband, Ron, for his patient and steadfast support throughout this creative journey. Thanks are also due to Karen English for looking over my references to the Islamic faith, to Larry Holben and Susan Hart Lindquist for reading the novel in manuscript, to Diane Matchek and again to Susan for dispensing comfort and courage in all weathers, and to Wesley Adams at Farrar, Straus and Giroux for true and faithful editing.